Joseph McGee Private Investigator: Book One

FRIENDS AT HOMELAND SECURITY

McGee Meets Federal Resistance

Carl Douglass

Neurosurgeon Turned Author Writes With Gripping Realism

PO Box 221974 Anchorage, Alaska 99522-1974
books@publicationconsultants.com—www.publicationconsultants.com

ISBN 978-1-59433-554-9
eISBN 978-1-59433-575-4
Library of Congress Catalog Card Number: 2015952491

Manufactured in the United States of America.

Dedication

To the people of the wild, Wild West and
a nod to the effete Easterners.

Disclaimer

All of the six novellas in the McGee Series are works of fiction and should not be construed as representing real persons, places, or events. Some names of real persons and places appear but only for the purpose of creating a setting in the real world or as a mention of historical circumstances. None of the real people or the real places were actually involved in the fictional portrayals found in these short books. All of the events described were created from the author's imagination.

Chapter One

My name is Joseph Patrick Aloysius Michael John McGee. Really. That moniker was a gift from my sainted mother—rest her soul—who was more Irish than the Fenians and more Catholic than the pope. She was very young when I came along, and as she could not make up her mind what to call her firstborn, she used all the names from some Irish ditty. Sometimes she even called me all of them when she was mad at me, but mostly she called me Joseph Patrick. Having such a peculiar name guaranteed that I would grow up tough—something in the order of being named "Sue" like the Johnny Cash song. I learned to fight in the first grade and earned my crooked nose and the right to be known only as McGee to everyone but my mother thereafter.

I am a private investigator who came by the profession in an unlikely way. Most PIs were former cops who either became unfit for further NYPD service or retired with a nice letter, a nice plaque, and a meager pension, and chose being a PI over being a security guard. I, on the other hand, knew what I wanted to be from my midteens. I got a degree in criminology at CUNY, graduating with honors after three years, and a law degree from Columbia. My first job was as a CSI for NYPD. That lasted three years; I quit because the pay was too low and the promotions too slow. I then worked as a criminalist for the FBI, specializing in ballistics and then banking fraud for a total of five years. I quit because I could no longer stomach the bureaucracy. PI work is not all that lucrative for most people, probably because they are just not suited for high-end work. My firm—McGee & Associates—does its share of nasty divorce dirt-digging and embezzlement work, but our real money comes from surveillance in corporate espionage cases, forensic accountancy, and in-depth investigations for the defense in high-profile criminal cases—usually murders.

The office of McGee & Associates Investigations is in midtown Manhattan, is clean and presentable with chrome and glass fixtures, and has no hand-painted signs by the proprietor—another set of differences between me and the lower class of PIs whom the real cops refer to as "bottom feeders." We don't advertise on TV or on billboards. My clients are largely rich, have serious issues with opponents; or, in criminal cases, they have vices to hide and important secrets to keep. Our policy is to provide the truth, and the clients who pay the bills are informed up front that we will not lie for them in or out of court, and we will give them all of what we discover and let them be the judge of how to use the information. We don't take bribes; anyone who does such a thing will be kicking rocks down the road half a minute after I learn that he or she does. Sometimes our clients balk at such pristine morality, but it has paid off over the two decades we have been in business.

I have two partners: Caitlin O'Brian, who has been with me for six months. Her former occupation was as one of New

York's finest, a homicide detective in the Central Investigation and Resource Division, Homicide Analysis Unit, before she ran afoul of her precinct captain. It seems there was a disagreement about who had the right to do what with which and to whom, and she decked him. To avoid unpleasantness of separation with its attendant negative publicity, Caitlin accepted a full pension and a nice letter of recommendation. She is a tough black Irish girl from the Bronx who had four brothers—a condition that lent itself to an early education in fighting. After finishing the academy and doing her rookie year, she obtained an associate degree in criminology specializing in bank fraud and handwriting analysis. That proved to be boring, so the feisty colleen moved to the homicide division of midtown Manhattan where I first met her.

My other partner is Ivory White, an unlikely name for the blackest man I ever met. He has something of a murky past about which I know everything, and no one else knows anything. He is—in the vernacular—the muscle of the organization. He is tall, athletic, bald, arrogant, and mean if needs be—and that is often the case in his line of work, perhaps best known by its euphemism—"special investigations." He does all of our personal security for high profile clients. For all of his martial arts and other physical skill sets, Ivory is extremely intelligent. He is a remarkable linguist who speaks six of the most useful languages of the 800 used by the citizens of the most densely populated city in the country if not the world.

I sign on for the Decklin Marcus case after his father— the investment banker, Howard Everhart Marcus—solicits my help. Decklin—the scion of the wealthy and influential family—was found dead in his uptown Manhattan apartment. Marcus senior does not accept that his son simply died from no cause. His death was untimely and unexpected. There was no suicide note, evidence of forced entry into his apartment, or indication of how he died. Toxicology was negative, and there were no signs of foul play. The young man was lying in what appeared to be peaceful repose on his living room couch. The ME ruled the death to have been due to unknown causes. An NYPD medical consultant concluded that the cause was likely to have been due to a sudden cardiac arrhythmia, even though there was no history of heart problems of any kind.

I was given a heads up about the case by a friend of mine in the detective division, Mary Margaret MacLeese, whose name is as Irish as mine—and she is in all ways more Irish than me. She does not agree with the benign cause of death opinion any more than does Decklin's father, but the department could not expend any more resources on an investigation that was going nowhere. Our association began when a New York detective named Martin Redworth was accused by IA of theft of drugs from an evidence box. My firm and I cleared Redworth—at the time a significant-other of Mary Margaret—and did it pro bono. From time to time, Mary Margaret and Martin repay me with useful tips, some help with information only obtainable from NYPD locked computer files, and by referring potential clients who might benefit from a more relaxed set of investigative rules and regulations than those imposed on the NYPD.

I put down the phone after getting everything I could from Howard Marcus, and signal Caitlin.

"Hey, Caitlin," I say as I move quickly toward the door, "want to take a break from your never-ending boredom?"

"Sure, boss, where to?"

"We have a new client. I'll fill you in as we go."

Going to Decklin Marcus's is by the corporation limousine—the only civilized way to get around in New York. Ed Rainer, our driver, was formerly one of our clients who had been accused of using excessive force with a pair of rowdies in the performance of his duty as a bouncer in a house of ill repute in the South Bronx, a streetcar suburb not quite close enough to Manhattan to be chic or safe. Two men were killed in that case: one died during the mini-riot that broke out when Ed succeeded in ejecting the drunken patron who was supported by his Irish hockey team pals, and the regulars in the place who respected and decided to assist Ed. Ed did not do the killing, but nobody with Irish blood believed that. Ivory killed the second man in the line of his duty as a security guard for Ed Rainer. Both men were cleared of any wrongdoing after Caitlin and her staff produced cellphone videos of both encounters. Ed was never actually charged with anything, but he credited our firm for having protected his freedom and saving his life. He is so loyal to the three of us partners that it is sometimes embarrassing. He is an excellent driver and an equally excellent addition to Ivory's crew of personal security providers.

I take Caitlin with me to the crime scene, if it is correct to call it that. I want to get her involved for her analytic skills and good common sense. We choose to look around the beautifully restored old brownstone apartment building in uptown Manhattan just off East 65th Street in the 100–130 blocks before going to interview the young man's parents. It is Caitlin's idea. She thinks it would be best for us to get some up-close-and-personal background before having to meet the parents cold to talk. The plastic yellow crime scene tape is still up at the four-bedroom condo when we arrive, even though the police are pretty much done with their search of the apartment—and of the case for that matter.

There are two minor hitches in our plan. First, it is illegal to cross crime scene tape unless you are police, from the district attorney's office, or from the medical examiners. Caitlin and I are none of those. We have not been to the Marcus's house in exclusive Gramercy Park yet, so we do not have a key to the door of Decklin's apartment. I am a strictly law-abiding citizen most of the time. The firm's brochure says so. However, I cannot say as much for my newest partner, Caitlin O'Brian, formerly an NYPD detective who was sworn to uphold the law. Without hesitation or any evidence that she was entering into an ethical and moral grey area, let alone the legal issues—Caitlin produces a lock pick set and has us in the door in a minute. I make a mental note to chastise her when an appropriate moment manifests itself, if I can remember my responsibility.

"Nice work, Caitlin," I say.

"Tweren't nuthin, boss. I wasn't one of New York's best-trained detectives for nothing. Let's get going on the detecting."

I am good at "detecting" in rooms where the police and CSIs have already had their turn. Still, I do not find anything of note. My young partner—in a neat little demonstration of one-upmanship—finds a clue.

Chapter Two

" I'm clear in here," I say to Caitlin after two hours of work in the kitchen and bathroom.

I have been painstaking in the extreme and came up with nothing. There are plenty of fingerprints, all of which had already been checked out by NYPD. I know that because I call Det. Mary Margaret MacLeese and insist that she owes me a favor. She insists that she and I are even, but she will check the fingerprints evidence from the apartment for me anyway.

"Just the usual suspects," she says, "three friends from work and half a dozen from school—all of which have good alibis. No terrorists, no serial killers, no bookies, no fallen women. Maybe the only thing of interest is that there were no prints for a girlfriend. We checked around, and there is no girlfriend. Incidentally, there is no evidence that he likes boys better."

"Well, thanks, Maggie ... I guess," I say.

"Sorry. I guess it's kind of 'Thanks for nothing,'" she says.

"Don't feel bad, Maggie, that just adds to the mystery.'"

"The mystery that got you—the great Shylock Holmes—hired on to show up the simpletons at robbery-homicide."

"That one, yeah. Anyway, thanks, my friend. I owe you one."

"I'll remember," she says.

I pack up my crime-scene kit and go look for Caitlin. She is in the second floor bedroom.

"I guess we're beat here. Cops didn't find anything and, for once, I can't find anything they missed. We might as well get on back to the office," I say.

"Not quite so fast, boss. I have something."

Caitlin looks animated. I have a sneaking hunch that she has one-upped me.

"What?" I ask her as she hunches over her laptop, waiting for something to pop up on a screen that is rolling facial images faster than anyone's eyes or brain can follow.

She gives me the wait-a-minute sign. A final message comes up: "NO MATCH."

"That doesn't look like 'something' very much," I comment.

That does not dampen her enthusiasm.

"It *is* something. I found a thumbprint on the window latch. I ran it through IAFIS, NCJRS, the Violence and Abuse Abstracts, and Interpol. Same answer every time, "NO MATCH." I even sent a little scraping to CODIS [Combined DNA Index System—FBI]."

It takes me a moment to recognize how much of a 'something' she has. There are very, very few individuals who have not been fingerprinted for something or other in their entire lives, and not just in the United States. Caitlin has covered most of the world in her electronic search.

"Who doesn't have a fingerprint record?" I muse out loud.

"Maybe a hayseed from Nebraska who never got into the military, never had any kind of a run-in with the cops, and never applied for a government, law enforcement, or school job—any school job at any educational level," Caitlin says.

"Maybe a spy with the deepest of the deepest cover."

"Even then, the CIA and the other unified intelligence organizations have been pretty willing to share the fingerprints of their employees when we ask nicely."

"I see where you're going," I say. "Somebody has to be flying way under the radar to have avoided being identified. IAFIS alone has seventy-one million criminal fingerprints, thirty million civil fingerprints, and almost seventy-five million terrorist subjects. Add to that the separate files from the cooperating—and that is almost everyone, everywhere—state and local governments, the military, mental hospital, and prison databases. The NCJRS [National Criminal Justice Reference Service] abstracts database has its own files on a couple of hundred thousand prints from the criminal and juvenile justice systems, drug control agencies, and the Violence and Abuse Abstracts database fingerprint records. It hardly seems possible that we could have someone that obscure opening a window in Decklin Marcus's bedroom."

"And not just any bedroom, McGee. This one opens out on to the fire escape."

"Hmm, hmmh," I hum wisely, having nothing better to add.

"Any rabbits in your hat, boss? We need one."

I have a bit of a serendipity moment.

"I know a guy," I say. "Well—kind of a guy. If my guy can't find this stealth B&E perp, then he or she is not going to be found by any easy electronic route."

"Who's your guy?" Caitlin asks.

"I don't want to seem either overly secretive or grandiose, but I really can't tell you that. It is literally a top secret."

Caitlin shrugs, "Okay, McGee. I hope your guy can find something for us. Otherwise we are up the proverbial creek for the time being."

"In the worst sort of way. This means that we are going to have to do what I hate most—knock doors; go to bars, restaurants, clubs; talk to people; and get real tired."

She sighs. "I guess we start in the neighborhood first."

"We'll have to get the whole team from McGee and Associates over here to Gramercy Park and start doing cop work," I say. "While they're assembling, I will give my guy a call."

Calling the director of the CIA is more than a bold move; it borders on criminal. I once worked on a very serious problem with Sybil Norcroft—the current director—when she was a special agent—a very special one. As the one who was called Gideon, she was in charge of an ultra-top secret task force assigned to find a mole. McGee and Associates participated in the vetting of suspects and in the field mission that resulted in the removal of double-agents who were selling state secrets to al-Qaeda. The problem was that only a very few people could persuade the Langley operator to put them through to the DCIA—people like the president, the DNI, the NSA, and the like.

I try twice to go the usual route. I ask to speak to the director and am firmly shunted elsewhere. To my chagrin, I remember that the operators only put calls through to specifically named individuals. I suck it up and then ask to speak to Sybil Norcroft. That all but set off police sirens and the sound of jack boots. It takes me several minutes to mollify the security officer who comes on the line instead of Dr. Norcroft. Then I do my most brazen thing: I ask for Gideon, S7A3N0D75#Marburg per PDD-3071—the director's most secret code from that counter-espionage mission.

"This is a secure line," comes Director Norcroft's soft but authoritative voice, "where did you get that code?"

Her voice is not so soft then.

"I'm sorry, Director. This is McGee," I say. "I know I shouldn't have used the code, but it is the only way to get through. I don't know anybody else, and I hope you might remember our association in the NCIS case."

My reference is to the NCIS officer and his superior, Vice Admiral Duncan Lloyd Jennings, DCNO [Deputy Chief of Naval Operations] who was also a heroin smuggler and long-term spy for al-Qaeda. I helped in his capture.

"You know that it is highly irregular for you to presume on our former association by using my very secret code. This must be an extremely important problem, McGee. Out with it."

She is obviously not in the mood for a little reminiscing chat; so, I waste no time in telling Dr. Norcroft the details.

Sybil Norcroft, MD, PhD, FACS, is no stranger to the real work of a field agent well beyond the comforts of her large office. She listens with a seasoned ear to everything I know about the Decklin Marcus case.

"What can I do for you, McGee?" she asks.

"I think I have a fingerprint that belongs to a deep-cover agent of some foreign power at the crime scene, Sybil, if I might presume to call you by your first name."

"I think we are beyond worrying about such trivialities as first names, McGee. I agree with you. Although evidence is lacking, it seems likely that this young man you have been investigating was murdered, and that he may well have been killed for some reason related to a foreign national's involvement. It is thin, but I have seen national security cases hang on thinner threads. I believe there are two things I can do for you. First, we can get over to the NCTC [National

Counterterrorism Center] and look at their database for fingerprints, et cetera. Then, we can work together to see if the owner of the thumbprint is anybody on the No-Fly list or other listing of personas non grata in the US and unfriendly to the things and people we value. Second, the Company has forensic and toxicology resources that even the NYPD and FBI don't have, especially when we are talking about real exotics.

"I'm talking about things like the Georgi Markov case. Do you remember that one?"

"Seems to ring a bell," I say, "but, no, I can't bring it to mind."

"Markov was a Bulgarian dissident in the communist era—late 70s—and was unforgivably loud about it. He got sick and complained to his doctors about having developed his illness after a man with an umbrella walked past him while he was crossing the Thames on Waterloo Bridge, and it seemed to Markov that he was hit in the leg with something. He was very precise about the day—September 7, 1978. I remember it because it was all over the news at the time of his death. At first, he ignored it as some sort of a sting or bite from a bug. Later, as he was dying, he told his doctors that he was sure that he had been poisoned. He had good reason to believe that because the *Darzhavna Sigurnost* [Bulgarian secret police] had made two previous verified assassination attempts on him.

"After he died, British authorities ordered an autopsy. The medical examiners found a tiny puncture wound on the back of Markov's right thigh; and, when they probed, they extracted a tiny—pinhead-sized—microengineered spherical metal ricin pellet."

"Boy, that is ingenious!" I say, meaning every word of the flattery. "I am going to have to study more history. You know, Sybil, you may be onto something."

"Ah, shucks," she says, "it's just my night-school education."

I had to laugh at the thought of the ultra-sophisticate Sybil Norcroft—consummate physician, renowned neurosurgeon, former surgeon general of the United States, international lecturer, and head of the most prestigious spy agency in the world—rubbing shoulders with the *untermenschen* at night school.

She gives me a self-deprecating smile before continuing.

"Is the boy . . . Decklin Marcus . . . is that right?"

"That's right. Good memory."

"Anyway, is his body still in the morgue?"

"He's in the city morgue—the one in the 400 block of 1st Avenue between 26th and 28th Aves, but they won't be holding him much longer."

"I can't appear to be involved, McGee. You'll have to get your NYPD detective friends to ask the OCME [Office of the Medical Examiner] to put a hold on it for a few more days. It will take a while to get the studies done."

"Does it matter that he's been dead for three days already?"

"I really don't know, but I doubt it. We can give it a try, at least."

"Thanks a million, Sybil. I definitely owe you a favor. Don't hesitate."

"I won't, McGee. I keep a little black book for such things. I'll call you tomorrow, and we'll go over to the NCTC and take a look in their private fingerprint files. I'm owed a few favors over there, and I know a guy—as we say—who can get a handle on a weird and wonderful poison if anyone can."

Chapter Three

I tell Caitlin and Ivory what I learned from "my guy" but not who she is, what position she holds, or in what agency. Close as we all are, I decide that they do not need to know that. I am to meet with the DCIA that afternoon, and together we are going to begin the serious work of my investigation. Director Norcroft would know everything every step of the way, but that could not be helped.

The team spreads out by twos and canvasses everyone and every place in Gramercy Park neighborhood to which they can gain access that morning. This neighborhood encompasses everything from New York's 17th to 22nd Streets and from east of Park Avenue South to Third Avenue. It was originally built around a beautiful private park—one of the perfectly kept green spots in the nation's most important city—in the nineteenth century. Getting into Gramercy Park is not for the *untermenschen* I had referred to in my conversation with Sybil Norcroft. The houses and apartment buildings surrounding the park are some of the most seriously coveted real estate in the world. Ownership is the only way to have a $500 passkey—

a total of 383 such keys in existence—to make it through the gates of the park. Rockefellers, Astors, Chelsea Clinton, and Julia Roberts live there, and the Morgan Library is nearby. The place is the very quintessence of "exclusive." Visitors—like McGee and associates—are not allowed to consume alcohol, smoke anything, ride a bicycle, or, heaven forbid, a motorcycle or anything resembling it, walk a dog, feed the birds and squirrels, play any form of ball, throw a Frisbee, or take a nap on the precisely manicured lawns.

"So, what do we do now?" Caitlin and Ivory ask when we come to the gates at the 23rd Street entrance on the north boundary.

I laugh.

"Oh, smarty pants, I suppose you know a 'guy,'?" Caitlin says with a mock peeved expression.

"I just happen to," I say, savoring another little piece of one-upmanship.

I had put Howard Everhart Marcus's landline at number 15 and cell numbers for him and his wife, Anne, into my iPhone when we first communicated about the death of their son, Decklin. A maid answers.

"Please tell Mr. or Mrs. Marcus that McGee is calling. I need to get into the park."

There was a moment of frost.

"I will see if the master or the mistress is receiving calls," she says, making an effort to ensure that her voice was in the proper nasal—or as we *untermenschen* would say, snooty—tone.

In less than a minute, Anne Marcus comes on the line.

"Good morning, Mr. McGee," she says. "Any news?"

"Not exactly, and not on the phone, Ma'am. My partners and I are at the gates. We have some news to communicate, and it must be direct; it's sensitive."

"I'll come myself," she says. "Which entrance?"

"23rd Street," I tell her.

She is there in less than five minutes. Even Ivory is impressed at my clout. He swears that he will never again make fun of me when I say "I know a guy."

The frost and the nasal intonation is gone from the maid when the three McGee and Associates private eyes arrive at the front door of the thirty-four-room colonial revival style mansion. Next door on the left is a house that is a National Historic Landmark, and the house on the right is an attractive smaller Tudor home that survived Prohibition by putting itself forward as a mortuary.

"Please have a seat, Mr. McGee, Mr. White, and Ms. O'Brian," Mrs. Marcus directs when we enter an elegantly appointed parlor.

The silent and almost invisible maid brings in a tray of obviously very expensive organic loose Hawaiian Natural Tea, steaming hot.

Anne Marcus is a handsome thirty-something blond woman—tall and patrician—who reminds me of Sybil Norcroft somewhat. But, where Mrs. Marcus is handsome, Dr. Norcroft is truly beautiful in an athletic sort of way. Both of them have striking blond hair—Dr. Norcroft's is almost certainly genetic, while Mrs. Marcus has had some work done. Mrs. Marcus is nervous and ill-at-ease, and it is obvious that she has been crying. No one could fault her for any of that. I had seen Sybil Norcroft on her worst day—the day she learned that her only child, Cerisse, had been kidnapped— and she never lost her poise. I have to say that both women seem quite down-to-earth for all of their worldly accomplishments and possessions.

"I hate to ask, Mr. McGee, because I know you're very busy; but could we wait for the news you are bringing until my husband can get here? I called him at work as soon as you and I hung up, and he said he could be here in less than fifteen minutes. I would feel more … I guess … secure, if he were here with me. I hope you understand," she says with a little quaver in her voice.

"Certainly, Mrs. Marcus. You are going through a most distressing time," I say as soothingly as I can. "Maybe we can have a little tour of the house while we wait."

It is probably the most beautiful home I have ever been in.

That pleases her both because of the compliments on the house which is her pride and joy, but also because it will give her something to do.

The tour includes only the main floor. There is enough original artwork on just that floor to grace a medium-sized city's best art museum. In the entryway hangs a masterwork by Pomm (just Pomm)—*The Story of Unspoken Courage*, a touching depiction of a fireman and a boy after 9-11. Hanging from the museum-like walls are notable and nearly priceless works by the German printmaker, Albrecht Durer—*The Hare*, painted in 1502—the English printmaker and poet William Blake; J. M. W. Turner's *Dolbadarn Castle*, painted in 1799; a Winslow Homer Civil War union camp scene; and oils by Albert Marie Adolphe Dagnaux, Alexander Pope, Americans Dennis Miller Bunker and Patricia Watwood, and the Italian Paolo Sala. The floors are covered with artwork as well: handwoven carpets from India, Pakistan, Morocco, and Syria—most of them more than 150 years old. Even the furniture is art: Michael Allison cabinets, a federal couch made by William Camp, and a hunter table and dining room table made by Deming & Bulkley.

When Mrs. Marcus moves momentarily out of earshot, Caitlin ventures the observation, "I could retire on the income from any five of the paintings, or even of the first floor furniture."

I shake my head in agreement. Ivory—ever the cool dude—acts as if he were in his element. I have to laugh, but I avoid facing Ivory when I do.

Howard Marcus's limo pulls up to the front entrance, and his chauffeur gets out and opens his door for him.

He meets his wife and the McGee Associates in the parlor and shakes hands all around. He is dressed in a $1,800 Saville Row suit with all the necessary trimmings. He is tall, lean, tan; and his hair—greying at the temples—was trimmed today, it would appear. I guess that his barber bill exceeds my rent. For all of that, he is as down-to-earth as his wife. Despite his inner turmoil, he makes an effort to make us feel comfortable.

"Thank you for coming, and thank you for taking our case, Mr. McGee. I know it seems unlikely that we can find out anything more than the police have. I think they have been most thorough; but Anne and I just can't accept that our perfectly healthy—and, may I say, beloved—son just keeled over dead. The autopsy showed nothing. There is no evidence of any disease or of foul play. Maybe we are just doting and bereaved parents, but my objective nature keeps pushing me to doubt. That's why we asked around and came up with a number of glowing references to your firm, Mr. McGee."

"Mr. Marcus, most people just call me McGee. I have too many names to come up with a single first name that is to my taste. I would appreciate it if you would call me McGee. And I can speak for my associates—Caitlin and Ivory."

"Happy to," Marcus says, "and we are Howard and Anne. I like to think that we can become friends; so, you will take personal stock in our problem and not just consider it another case."

"Thanks, Howard. We have already gotten personally involved. Objectively, we have been busy and have come up with some information that may shine a light on the death of your son. This afternoon I will be going to an institution that specializes in exotic identification data and some about criminal activities that cannot be accessed routinely. Caitlin and Ivory will continue to canvass the neighborhood. We would appreciate it if you could give your neighbors a call to grease the skids for us. We are not likely to get past the butler if you don't," I tell him.

"Consider it done. We will sit down with our staff and get started as soon as you leave us. If I may ask, where are you going to get your exclusive information?"

I was afraid he would ask that.

"I'm sorry, Howard…Anne, but I really cannot share that with you. The stakes are too high, and my friends are extremely skittish. Please try and understand. We will share everything we learn except for identifying our sources. It is possible that you may not like some of what we find as we go along, but our promise is the truth and nothing but. We don't sugarcoat things, and we don't avoid unpleasantness in our investigations if it comes up."

"Good, McGee. That's how I run my business. When or how often will we hear from you?"

"Once a day at seven in the evening, if that fits your schedule. If we get a break, we will let you know immediately."

"Sounds like Wolf News," said Anne with a wan smile at her attempt at a little humor.

I speak for the McGee associates, "We need information from you—everything you know about your son, about his friends, his enemies, his acquaintances at work and in school…everything. Let us see his yearbooks, any files of newspaper clippings, all of his diplomas, and any secrets. This is no time for daintiness. We have reason to believe that all is not kosher in his death, and we intend to get to the bottom of the conundrum wherever our investigation takes us.

"I have to get away now to see my source. You can trust Caitlin and Ivory for their thoroughness and discretion. Thank you for the hospitality."

The maid shows me to the door.

The last thing I hear before making my exit is Ivory asking, "Please tell me your whereabouts on the evening of your son's death, Thursday the ninth."

"Do you really think we need to have alibis?" Marcus says.

As the door was closing, I hear Ivory say what I expected him to say, "Yes."

Caitlin uses up a couple of her personal markers to get the OCME to hold the body of Decklin Marcus for another ten days. Sybil Norcroft's office arranges with the medical examiner himself to have one of the CIA forensic pathologists come to the City Mortuary to go over the autopsy with the ME to see if anything new could be found—like a small hole in the back of his leg.

I meet Sybil in a Wendy's in McLean, Virginia, at ten. I make a serious effort to be there earlier than the DCIA; so, I will not queer any chance I have to get our information—no "The traffic was brutal," or "My alarm didn't go off," for this meeting. A definite indicator that this meeting is going to be clandestine is that Sybil arrives in a six-year-old Chevy somewhat the worse for wear, and she is dressed in casual clothes and wears a broad-brimmed hat.

"Nice hat," I say with a smile.

"It's from the prop department," Sybil responds with an equal smile. "Let's get to the NCTC. I got us an appointment—on the QT—with my guy in the Forensic Database Section at ten twenty."

I love all of the "guys" who keep popping up like angels more or less out of nowhere. It is proving to be very convenient.

The NCTC center is one of the divisions of the ODNI [Office of the Director of National Intelligence]. It is responsible for national and international counterterrorism efforts—the latter being the reason for our quest. The center is based in a huge blocky X-shaped complex in McLean, Virginia, better known locally as "Liberty Crossing" off the Dulles Airport Access Road and 267 near Tysons Corner. The complex is located in a beautiful green-wooded area, but the building is a mass of grey stone and small, unexciting windows. We enter the complex through the west gate—the Director of National Intelligence entrance—using the magic of Sybil's credentials and the added bonus of having an appointment with a known NCTC officer.

The Forensic Database section and lab are on the sixth floor of the west building. I am not cleared to go to any of the levels below the main ground floor. We are frisked by a male and a female security officer before obtaining our passes and then take the express elevator to the sixth floor where we are met by another pair of security guards. If you like that sort of thing, the NCTC building is a great place to get your jollies. I, personally, just tolerate it as a necessary evil of my job.

John Smedley, the chief of the Forensic Database Section, meets us as soon as we are able to get inside his castle walls. He and Sybil go way back, apparently.

"Hi, Sybil. Sorry for all of the security stuff. It gets old."

"Hi, John. It's about the same as over at the Company," Sybil says and makes of all sweet accord with one of her winning smiles.

"I got the fingerprint files from your office this morning. Our computer wizards have already run them through our databases—emphasis on the plural. It took a bit, but we did get a hit and a very interesting one," Smedley announces.

I stand by like a wooden Indian statue outside a cigar store while the two grand poobahs have their talk. Finally, Sybil remembers me and makes an introduction.

"Oh, yes—sorry, McGee, you need to be introduced. Dr. John Smedley, chief of the database for counterterrorism, allow me to present the notable private detective, Joseph P.A.M.J. McGee. Nobody can remember all of his Christian names. We all just call him McGee," Sybil says with a wry grin.

We two men shake hands.

"Call me John," the chief says. "Okay if we stay informal and I call you McGee? I am familiar with your outfit—McGee and Associates, right?"

"Correct on both counts," I say.

Then, we get down to work.

"This is what we found, Sybil, McGee. The print is a good one, fortunately. It is from the thumb of a real nasty known to certain highly selected members of the counterterrorism world as "Waterloo" for some reason. His real name—or more likely one of his known aliases—is Viachaslau Mazurkiewicz, a Byelorussian mercenary wetwork agent. You two have stumbled on a print that could not have been expected for any proper reason in the United States, and could not bode well for anybody in a place where his print is found."

"Nice work, John—thanks," Sybil says sincerely.

"Maybe not, Sybil. Look at this."

John's computer screen opens to a large insignia of the United States Department of Homeland Security with a flashing message, "ACCESS DENIED. CLASSIFIED TOP SECRET."

"Hmmh," Sybil hums subtly.

Unaccustomed to subtlety, I barge right in, "You have to have gotten around that little impediment, John. *That* is nice work."

Both John and Sybil give me an indulgent smile—one reserved for the family's awkward but harmless teenager.

"And beyond your need to know," Sybil says, giving me a bit of a look.

I nod my understanding and the acceptance of the implicit scolding.

"Well—a long story made short—we did get some information on him. You can have the redacted printout, but you cannot tell anyone how you got it. In fact, it would be much the best if you didn't tell anyone anything about the information or its source."

"Mum's-the-word," I say clumsily.

Sybil gives John the in-group acceptable nod.

"You can read the stuff at your leisure and in a secure place— I presume—but I have to warn you that while you will learn things about this consummate thug, there is nothing in here that relates to your victim or to the United States at all, for that matter. He doesn't seem to hold any official intelligence position. As far as we know he is a merc whose services are available to the highest bidder. He has a near-perfect record: he gets an assignment, and someone sloughs his mortal coil or simply disappears."

"Any hope that we will be able to establish that he killed Decklin Marcus or how?"

All of the geopolitics aside, that is my main *raison d'état* for being here.

"My assistant and I are meeting Jack Tamaguchi at the New York mortuary this afternoon to go over the autopsy results—hands-on—and to get tissue and bone marrow samples from the body for toxicology. They still have blood, urine, stomach contents, brain tissue, and segments of bowel we can work with. I'm pretty confident that if it was poison, we'll find it. It'll take a few days to get all of the results back; this is not a television CSI show where the whole thing gets wrapped up in an hour with a third of the time being taken up by 'product reviews' as Madison Avenue puts it these days."

"We appreciate everything," Sybil tells him. "We'll be patient."

I feel impatient but keep quiet. I am sure that any more of my extraneous comments and enthusiasms will not be appreciated at this juncture.

John continues, "Look, you guys. You are playing with some heavy hitters. Homeland Security does not take kindly to interference, meddling, or hacking into their affairs. If your Decklin Marcus is part of some investigation of theirs, you can bet that you will have a visit. McGee, I suspect that a couple of large and unsmiling HS special agents will pay you a visit in the very near future. Sybil, I think you are likely to hear from Secretary Carter from Homeland or maybe even the president. Just a heads up.

"One thing to note in the report I gave you is that nice Mr. Mazurkiewicz—or whatever his real name is—has been known to be in the employ of the *Solntsevskaya Bratva*. He might even have been involved in the sniper killing of 'Grandpa Hassan' a few years ago."

I make my face into a question mark.

"The Russian Mafia … and 'Grandpa Hassan' was reputed to be the king of the mob. He was killed in a power struggle within the mob," Sybil explains.

"Heavy hitters," I say. "What has our poor little rich boy gotten himself into?"

"That will be the question of the day, and presumably what your current employers are going to want to know," Sybil says.

"They did say that they wanted the unvarnished version. I'll wait until the toxicology data are back before I start giving them the details," I answer.

Chapter Four

On the fourth and eighth days after our supposedly secret visit to the NCTC, two important things happen. The first—on day four—is that John Smedley from the NCTC and Jack Tamaguchi, the Chief Medical Examiner for the City of New York, repeat the autopsy on young Decklin Marcus. That produces very probative results immediately and more convincing findings once the toxicology results return from the NCTC Forensic Database Section. The second memorable thing—four days later—is a visit meant to instill an enduring impression on me and my associates.

Ivory White and I attend the second autopsy while Caitlin continues to flesh out the lives of the Marcus family and their friends and contacts. The original autopsy had been done exactly according to the book, and no fault could be found in that. The original tox screen was thorough and standard and even included a few extras. There is no question about the results of either the autopsy or the toxicology evaluation.

The second autopsy is about small things—attention to very fine detail. Dr. Smedley literally goes over Decklin's skin with a magnifying glass. He shaves Decklin's armpits and groins. That produces the first and only anatomical finding. When he finds it, Dr. Smedley calls the rest of us over to have a look through his magnifying glass. None of us, including Dr. Tamaguchi, would have ever found the lesion.

"You see that little pinpoint hole in the skin? It was completely obscured by his pubic and upper thigh hair. I can tell you that it occurred antemortem."

"What occurred, doc?" Ivory asks.

"I think I can be quite precise but not able to swear to it until the tox screen comes back. This is an injection site; a tiny needle—probably a 30 gauge—was used to inject a large concentrated dose of a rapidly acting neurotoxin and cardiac toxin like TTX. Mr. Marcus was almost certainly paralyzed immediately; and, presuming that the dose was high enough, within minutes he likely suffered a complete respiratory paralysis and a ventricular arrhythmia which killed him instantly. Although there is a tiny area of reddening around the puncture site indicating pressure from the tip of the syringe, there are no other signs of struggle or defensive acts on Mr. Marcus's part. The scenario I just described is the best explanation for the extant facts: no physical signs of struggle, negative regular toxicology screen, no organ damage on the internal anatomical evaluation, and nearly sudden and unexpected death in a healthy young man."

"I know something about TTX, Dr. Smedley, but how about a tutorial to teach or refresh those of us who wouldn't have thought of this?" Sybil asks.

Both pathologists contribute to the "tutorial," which is absolutely fascinating and eye-opening to both McGee and Ivory and a serious review for Sybil.

Dr. Tamaguchi leads off, glad to have an opportunity to appear to be something more than just a spectator in his own domain.

"TTX [Tetrodotoxin] is an extremely potent sodium channel blocker from Tetraodontiformes, a marine order that includes such diverse species as pufferfish, balloon fish, porcupinefish, ocean sunfish or mola, triggerfish, and horseshoe crab. Federal standards list the LD_{50} dose which produces a 50 percent mortality rate for a 170 pound man to be something on the order of 25 milligrams—nine ten thousandths of an ounce—if taken by mouth, and only eight to twenty-five micrograms if injected. The toxin has a very narrow therapeutic index and is almost always fatal when given in high doses. An assassin with access to refined TTX could just as easily inject a large dose as a small one. Dr. Smedley and I think the departed victim received something on the order of four MLDs [Minimum Lethal Dosages]. Mr. Marcus didn't have as much of a chance as the proverbial snowball in hell."

Ivory White interrupts again, "Sorry to interrupt your flow, doc, but isn't this the stuff the voodoo witch doctors in Haiti add to their potions to create zombies?"

Tamaguchi laughs. "It has been suggested by would-be 'experts,' but there is no evidence. Most potions—which are powdered mixtures of any number of insects, prescription and recreational drugs, and alcohol—have been shown not to have any TTX usually, and if present, to be in miniscule and nonlethal doses."

"Oh," says Ivory, "thanks."

Dr. Smedley continues, "This is the poison best known for causing fugu poisoning from the consumption of the Japanese delicacy, pufferfish. You have to know what you are looking for in order to get the correct studies. Once you stumble onto the idea that this could be fugu, the lab problem is not particularly difficult. Tetrodotoxin may be identified and quantified in serum, whole blood, and/or urine to confirm the diagnosis of poisoning. Our NCTC Forensic Database Section lab has the mass spectrometrometers and gas and liquid chromatographic separation equipment necessary for the forensic investigation of fatal overdosages. I am convinced that we are on the right track. It is a pleasure working with Dr. Tamaguchi. I will keep all of you posted as the results come in. Good detective work, by the way."

Sybil Norcroft and I give each other a small appreciative nod.

Four days later, Dr. Smedley calls Dr. Tamaguchi and the DCIA with his report.

"We were right; I am my usual modest self when I report this. But I have to say that the NCTC lab geeks went a step further. They established the manufacturing process of the injectable poison used. You may not know but the pufferfish and other TTX producers do not actually make the poison. Instead, it is produced by some bacteria which are symbiotic with the fish's cells and chemical makeup. In this case, the lab proved that a mixture of refined cultures of *Pseudoalteromonas tetraodonis*, and some species of *Pseudomonas* and *Vibrio* were used. That made an extraordinarily intense and rapidly acting toxin."

"How did this guy, Viachaslau Mazurkiewicz, come by such a sophisticated poison?" Sybil asks Dr. Smedley.

"That is the best question for detectives to ask. I can tell you this much: he did not come up with the idea himself, and he did not make the toxin himself or in his garage lab. This required university-level microbiologists using top-of-the-line research facilities and culture materials, and a lot of time to get the job done. I am of the opinion that this had to be a national project, since the costs would be prohibitive, and the availability of qualified personnel would be beyond the reach of any amateur manufacturer or highly knowledgeable and qualified assassin, however clever. So far as I know, only US, Russian, PRC, or UK lab facilities have all of the necessary ingredients."

"And that says nothing about motive. I presume that if we can find the motive, that will lead us to the culprit and to his or her country and laboratory," Sybil says with determination.

"Likely so, Madam DCIA. I would appreciate being kept in the loop. This is certainly a fascinating case and probably one that we will write up when the denouement is reached."

"I will be more than happy to let you know what we know. For now—and probably for the next thirty years—this will have to remain top secret."

Sybil calls me the same day.

"We have the toxicology report back, McGee. Your suspicions are altogether well-founded, and the experts' concepts are likewise right on."

She explains everything Dr. Smedley told her.

I ask her what she thinks was the scenario of the killing itself.

"I have gone over this with my two closest confidants—who, incidentally, are a couple of the nicest guys who ever boarded an innocent ship and scuttled it after robbing all of the passengers, raping all of the women, then killing every person on board—and they agreed on a plausible scenario to fit all of the facts.

"Lacking any defense wounds and the great care taken to place the tiny needle hole in the most obscure location possible, this is how they think it went down: probably two killers gained access into Decklin's apartment without having to resort to forced entry. One of them—probably Mazurkiewicz—got behind our victim and put him in a Brazilian jujitsu choke hold called the *mata leão* [kill the lion]. Are you familiar with it?"

"Yes. I have had some Brazilian jujitsu training myself," I reply, fully riveted by the scenario I can now envision all too well.

"The evil beauty of the hold is that it is quick. The victim does not strangle; so, he does not thrash around. He goes to sleep within half a minute and is rendered insensate and unable to defend himself. The hold leaves no marks. Mazurkiewicz then pulled down his pants, felt for the femoral artery pulse, and injected the sophisticated TTX solution directly into the arterial flow. With a presumably very large dose, Decklin likely did not wake up or suffer. He probably had a fatal ventricular arrhythmia almost immediately. Mazurkiewicz then made sure that there was no sign of blood, redressed Decklin, and put him on his couch; so, anyone but a highly suspicious expert forensic pathologist having access to a very sophisticated laboratory would come to the conclusion that this was some sort of fluke death—a cardiac arrhythmia in a healthy young man. It does occur, especially in athletes."

"Thanks a million, Sybil. We will get on this today. Fortunately for us the Marcuses are made of money, which enables us to do whatever is necessary to get the answers."

I arrive home late that evening after putting together a full report to give to the Marcuses. I am tired enough just to sit with my wife and watch Jay Leno for an hour then the late news before nodding off to sleep. The Marcuses can wait until tomorrow.

The rest is restorative, and I am bright-eyed and bushytailed when I walk into my Manhattan office at seven thirty in the morning, ready to round up the troops and get them headed in the directions I need them to go.

My office manager is the only other member of the staff in the office that early. She looks anxious and not like herself.

I look into her face, squint, then ask, "Hey, Vera, what's up? You look like you just lost your puppy."

Vera does not answer—just angles her head and body toward my office and raises her hands in a gesture of surrender. That cannot be the harbinger of anything good, I think.

As soon as I step into my private office, four men in dark suits, white shirts, red power ties, sturdy soft-soled black shoes, and opaque aviator sunglasses march into my path. They all have short military cuts; they are all big and altogether fit; and the nerves to create a smiley face appear to have been surgically removed. They are obviously clones manufactured by the federal government. They could be more obvious if they had "FEDERAL AGENT" tattooed on their foreheads.

"What?" I ask.

I was about to ask, "Who?" as well, but the oldest of the clones peremptorily and impatiently interrupts me.

"We'll ask the questions, Mr. McGee. As a matter of fact, we'll do almost all of the talking in this brief little get-together we are going to have."

I am still feeling put-off and feisty; so, I ask the "Who?" question anyway.

He ignores me.

"This is the way it's going to be, McGee. I talk, you listen. I learn, you stay in the dark. First thing, you tell me everything there is to know about Decklin Marcus and what you have dredged up about that unfortunate boy who died of natural causes and nothing else. Second, you give us all of your records and then you stay out of the Marcus affair…way out…and forever. Third, you don't share anything with the Marcuses, NYPD, or any federal office. Did you get that, or do you want me to go over it again real slow so that you can get it?"

He looks at me like he is talking down to a six-year-old schoolboy and a moron to boot.

"Creds," I say.

He looks at me like he is a mean principal looking down at a miscreant boy. His usually placid frown becomes more on the malevolent side.

"Shut up!" he says.

"No," I say. "This is my office, and I call the shots. First, I see the creds; then I find out why you are invading my space; then, maybe—or maybe not—I talk about what I know. I'll decide."

Two of the heavies standing behind the older agent take two menacing steps forward—close enough that we can almost rub noses. At that moment, Ivory White starts to walk into my office, obviously having been directed there by my eavesdropping office manager. There are only four of them, and I am afraid that Ivory might take it into his head to put a hurt on them—and that would be unseemly—so I motion for him to come in but to keep his distance for the time being.

"That your thug?" Older Man asks, disrespecting Ivory—which is not usually a wise thing to do according to my observation of how he handles such things.

Ivory's face loses its usual placidly friendly countenance, and he advances close enough to become part of the inner circle. It is tense. The four agents are used to being obeyed promptly; Ivory is used to being respected constantly; and I generally do not like being bullied in my own bailiwick.

"Time for you to leave," I announce to Older Man and hiss it enough to spray a bit of saliva into his too-close face.

The agent who has been standing off from the other three now advances. He is fingering a bulge in his left armpit, and I am pretty sure that he does not have an itch. It is getting tenser.

Just to throw a little more gas on the fire, I call out to my manager, "Hey, Vera, Ivory and I are being accosted by people who won't leave when asked to do so politely. Please call security ... no, strike that. Get NYPD up here. We inoffensive citizens are being assaulted by federal officers under the color of authority."

She pirouettes crisply and starts back to her desk and her telephone.

Older Man breaks the tension, "Assaulted?" he asks, incredulously.

"Yes, Agent. It's a fine point in criminal law that you likely skipped over in FBI school or whichever night school you attended. Assault is a verbal attack; battery is when you resort to touching or other physical violence. Am I to interpret your assault as a preliminary to battery?"

My voice is intentionally insulting—more so than I want it to be, but I am mad—and intend to have my adversary understand that his condescension toward me is mutual.

"So, which is it to be? NYPD or your creds and reasons, or you just leave. Take your pick," I say in a slightly more moderated tone.

Vera's hand is poised over her phone.

There is an angry pause, complete with ozone in the air— the sort that one imagines in a Mexican stand-off.

Older Man thinks for a moment, then says, "We're special agents of Homeland Security. I think you get my message. Back off."

I realize it is repetitive, but I tell him again, "Creds."

He grits his teeth and turns to his fellow agents and orders, "Back off for the moment."

All three of them remove their noses from the proximity of my nose, take their hands away from their gun holsters, and back away three steps.

I nod to Ivory, and he backs away two steps.

With almost theatrical reluctance, Older Man reaches into his jacket pocket and produces a standard federal cred-pack and flips it open for a second.

"Keep it open until I can read it," I demand.

Even more reluctantly, he does it until I am satisfied.

"Thank you for your courtesy, Special Agent," I say sweet as saccharine, and sincerely keeping to my motto for such situations always to be sincere whether you mean it or not.

"Stuff it, smart…," he starts to say, but evidently thinks better of completing the not necessarily complimentary word. "Like I said, back all the way off the Marcus case. Go peek in windows or bug some adulterer. Whatever. It will go down hard for you if you interfere again now that you have been officially warned."

Knowing better, I press it anyway, "Why? Why is Homeland Security interested in the unfortunate and untimely demise of a pleasant young man?"

"Don't play the buffoon, McGee. Just get the message. We won't tolerate your interference again. Today's meet is a friendly request. Tomorrow will go hard for you. Now step out of my way and get your thug to do the same thing. Oh, I do know a little about the law. The penalties for assaulting a federal officer are serious. Don't even think about it."

Much as I enjoy our little tête-à-tête, I do not think it wise to press my luck any further. I stand aside and nod to Ivory to do the same.

Chapter Five

The staff meeting starts at eight o'clock as usual, just after the four special agents of Homeland Security leave the building as unobtrusively as they came in.

The unspoken—and then the spoken—question on the lips of everyone in the office is, "What was all of that about?"

I have to confess that I have no idea, but have no intention of "backing-off" as I was ordered. I had had a crawful of orders when I worked for the FBI and then for the CIA. I am not a "take-orders" kind of a guy, and that is why I set up my own shop. Ivory White never took an order in his life, and I like him for that.

Caitlin asks the most salient question, "What have we gotten ourselves into?"

"That's the question of the day, Caitlin," I say, "and I, for one, am absolutely intrigued. This case is looking like a doozy with national and international implications. I want to find the answers even if we don't ever get paid. That okay with the rest of you guys?"

Everyone in the firm nods agreement, and Ivory snarls with venom, "I don't like being kicked around in my own space by my own government, and not being able to kick back. You bet I want to know things, but in the end of this I want to kick somebody hard enough that he has to button his pants around his neck because that'll be where his butt's gonna be."

There is general agreement on that score.

"All right, here are some assignments; so, we can keep focused. I'll fill Director Norcroft in. Caitlin, please get hold of Mary Margaret MacLeese and Martin Redworth—your NYPD pals. I think we need to bring them onboard. Ivory, how about you dig hard into young Decklin's activities? Consult the denizens of the dark and see what you can find that the boy wanted to hide. David, get your guys in IT to find every little thing about father Marcus, mother Anne, and the Global Investment Bank. See if you can turn up anything hinky. Be careful, but get into the *Solntsevskaya Bratva* phone and electronic messaging system. There has to be a solid connection to Decklin or his parents somewhere in there. Remember, they're good—and they're violent. Cover your tracks," I tell them.

"Hey, boss, that's like telling Werner Von Braun how to light a match," David Harger says, and we adjourn the meeting with an appreciative laugh.

I do some paperwork while Caitlin makes the calls. The NYPD detectives are more than happy to join us and agree that it all has to be very hush-hush. Their careers will be in the toilet if they get crosswise with Homeland Security or they proceed against the ultra wealthy Marcus clan with insufficient evidence. Caitlin makes an appointment with Howard and Anne Marcus for lunch. She suggests Loop, a reasonable and inexpensive sushi place on East 21st and Third Avenue, knowing that the sushi is good; and the rest of the food is no better than middling; and it is Filipino. She grits her teeth and tells Anne that we will pay. Anne agrees to the meet for lunch, but begs off going to Loop because Howard is allergic to fish—Caitlin could almost hear Anne's nose crinkle up at the idea of going to a cheap place—and Anne makes a counteroffer that we meet at Gramercy Tavern on East 42nd and 20th between Park Avenue and Broadway and will accept no argument about them paying. That is a good thing, because the tavern is one of the most pricey in all of New York—a four-$$$$ rating costing like eighty bucks a plate.

Mrs. Marcus suggests that we meet at eleven thirty to avoid the lunchtime rush, and because we would have to make a reservation for noon. Reservations involve a month's wait and no exceptions, even for Gramercy's elite. Caitlin readily agrees, and Ed drives us there in the limo.

The place is beautiful, light, and airy. We are greeted with a heavenly spicy smell as soon as we walk in. The Marcuses had gotten there just before we do and already have seats centered around a wood-burning grill. The unspoken rule among the gentry is no business until dessert and coffee; so, we all enjoy great food and even better service. Caitlin whispers at one point that she could get used to going out to where the elite meet to eat. I nod my enthusiastic agreement. The cuisine is American Nouveau—a learning experience for Caitlin. She starts with barely warmed vegetables covered with olives, pine nuts, herbed ricotta, and anchovy garlic paste, and fills the leftover space in her stomach with grilled monkfish—which is a hearty solid white fish that tastes like lobster. The fish is covered with small lightly browned flowerets of cauliflower, raisins, and curry. I choose fish croquette and mixed green salad with smoked oyster sauce for my appetizer, and butternut squash lasagna topped with hen-of-the-woods mushrooms and kale on the side as my entree. We are all too full for dessert or even for one of their specialty gourmet coffees. The Marcuses—slim, patrician, and fit—have only appetizers: he has roasted beets with kohlrabi, sherry vinaigrette, and sunflower seeds, while she has baked Long Island clams. No dessert, of course. They do have large steaming cups of black civet coffee—the most expensive in the world—and a true gourmet treat, since one has to get over the knowledge that it is made with the excreta of coffee berry-fed Asian cats.

The host opens the business. "All right, McGee and Caitlin, what have you got?"

I leave out the meeting with the DCIA but otherwise tell Howard and Anne pretty much everything. I also avoid telling them about the scrutiny we are in the process of putting on their lives.

"This Russian mafia figure means several things, Howard and Anne," I say by way of conclusion, "not the least of which is danger. I don't know for sure that you are in danger, but I suggest that you review your home security system and hire security guards around the clock even at the bank. Eat at home—only fresh food that you buy yourself or eat at restaurants chosen at random and without making reservations. Avoid public transportation and crowds. Don't allow anyone—even your secretaries or security people—to know what meetings you elect to attend. There's a saying out west, 'Trust everyone, but brand your cattle.' That's a good motto for you guys while our investigation is ongoing.

"One last thing: it is obvious that we are getting in over our heads what with Homeland Security taking a serious interest and ordering us to back off. So we have arranged to share the investigation with two detectives from the Manhattan Homicide Unit. The chief of D's is okay with that; so, we are staying kosher. You will eventually meet Detectives MacLeese and Redworth. They are going to need full access to your financial and telephone records—okay with you?"

Howard had been expressionless until my last sentence, but then he flinches and turns pale. He quickly recovers his composure—an excellent trait for a serious negotiator.

"I cannot allow bank business to be compromised, McGee. This involves more than just me; and our customers, clients, and the board of directors will never permit it, even for the purpose of getting to the bottom of our son's murder. I presume that the NYPD detectives are as discreet as you are, but there will have to be some careful negotiation on this subject," he says with finality.

It seems telling to me that he does not look me in the eyes when he says it.

"Sure. Thanks for the cooperation. We will work around the privacy issues."

"We have never had a personal security force take care of us, McGee," Anne Marcus says. "Can you arrange that?"

"We have an excellent man in charge of personal security. His name is Ivory White, and he will arrange all of the details. He is persnickety about his responsibilities; so, please do what he asks you to do. It will all be in your best interest."

On the way back to the office in the limo, Caitlin asks me, "Hey, McGee, did you see Howard's reaction when you told him he would have to have his business, e-mail, and telephone, etcetera, carefully evaluated and monitored?"

"Sure did. I was not really sure but that he might faint."

"Something to tuck into the back of our minds, I think," she says. "Now what?"

I say let's have a talk with Mary Margaret and Martin over at One Police Plaza. Our forensics accountancy is pretty good, but we need better. I think we are going to get further on this puzzle by following the money trail than any other way.

"Let me do that," I say, "and you do whatever is necessary to nail down the whereabouts of our alleged murderer, Viachaslau Mazurkiewicz. He is going to link the money to the string puller; and together, they are going to make our case for us."

"I'm all right with doing that, but I tell you this: something is rotten in Gramercy Park, or at least the Marcuses are more connected to the death of their son than they are telling," Caitlin responds.

"My hunch agrees with yours; but we don't have any evidence; and we can't get anything useful by squeezing them. Let's see where the forensics take us."

Caitlin gets hold of Mary Margaret who was willing to see us on short notice. Ed gets us to the lower Manhattan location of One Police Plaza in record time. Her office is on the seventh floor; and Caitlin—ever the fitness FemaNazi—makes us walk up the stairs. Martin Redworth is already sitting in front of Mary Margaret's desk when we get there.

"Come in and shovel the papers off a chair; so, you can take a seat," Mary Margaret says with a winning smile. "What can I do for the world-famous private eyes today?"

I take the lead, "Mary Margaret, Martin, we have a fairly good early working idea of what might be going on in the murder case of Decklin Marcus. We are pretty sure that there is more to the Marcuses than meets the eye. We asked Decklin's father, Howard, to let us see the bank records where he is involved, but he quickly turned coy. We need the big bad cops to order a full forensic accountancy. The answers are going to come from there. I am all but certain of that."

"What about you, Caitlin?" Martin asks.

"I couldn't agree more. We can't know too much about the Marcuses."

"What about that Russian mobster guy? How does he fit into the big picture?" queries Mary Margaret.

"Besides being the probable killer, we don't know enough about him—or about the Marcuses, for that matter—to be able to answer your question. Our office is going to follow that thread with all we have," I tell her. "And we would really appreciate it if the homicide unit would go after the Marcus parents. We have to be able to work with them—Howard Marcus brought the case to us, after all. That said, we won't get in your way; it is your case, but I think a division of labor will get us where we want to be. I am sure we need to get at the bank numbers before they 'accidentally' get lost as Nixon's secretary has always maintained about the missing Watergate tapes."

"We'll get a search warrant this morning and be in their house and in the bank this afternoon. I have a small hunch that your federal friend is likely to get roped in sooner or later as well. By the way, anything more come of the visit from your Homeland Security friends?"

"Not yet about the Homeland Security thugs. We'll keep you posted. We'll let you go and get at your investigation. Why don't we meet for lunch up near Gramercy Park tomorrow noon and share successes?"

"Ah, yes, that's the old McGee—the eternal optimist."

She stands up and, by unspoken mutual consent, the meeting is over.

Chapter Six

At quarter after four in the afternoon, David Harger, the IT guy, comes to my office.

"Hi, boss. I have a little something on the Marcuses. Seems that Howard keeps a separate stash of burner phones in an apartment he maintains in the Bronx. At first I thought it was just another pied-à-terre, but there's no evidence of hanky-panky on the transcripts of the conversations, which are few, short, and to the point. There was a little break-in at that location, it seems, and some people got a look around—can't say who."

I roll my eyes and laugh.

"Let's just say that the break-in did not get reported—and never will. There were several interesting things about father Howard's secret apartment. First, there is no bed in the entire place. Second, there are no cooking facilities; and the bathroom is spotless as if it has rarely, if ever, been used."

"Any records—anything we can use?" I ask him.

"Not exactly. There was something that might turn out to be worthwhile, though."

"And?" I push to get David to move along.

"There was a receipt for a box of burner phones. Unfortunately, the receipt did not match any of the Marcuses."

"And probably was a phony signature anyway," I say with some discouragement in my voice.

"Hang on," David said. "There's more. The signature on the receipt was that of a woman named Rachel Donovan."

"Name doesn't ring a bell. Is it fake?"

"Sort of," David said in his exasperatingly slow midtown accent.

My face shows my annoyance. I do not have to say anything.

"The fake part is that the handwriting of the signer is quite obviously that of a man. The true part is that such a person does exist. Evidently, our burner phone purchaser must have thought that it would only attract suspicion if the name and the address were fake. Even the store owner required photo ID—that's a recent New York law just appearing on the books. Apparently, the man who was signing the woman's name was able to swipe the card past the relatively uncomprehending shop owner's eyes. We checked the name. It belongs to a woman who, in fact, does live at the address on the receipt. It was not until we dug a little deeper that we found that the woman's name—which meant nothing to us at first—was that of a sister of one of Howard Marcus's bank partners. She is the widow of a Gulf War vet who died in the conflict, which accounts for her having an unfamiliar name. We in IT are presuming that the obscurity was intentional. It happens that she dotes on her brother and, in fact, depends on him to enhance her otherwise fairly skimpy income."

"Names?" I ask.

"Oh, yeah. Sister is Marilyn Woodworth—her married name—and the bank partner is Angus McTavish, a naturalized citizen from Scotland who moved to the US nearly twenty years ago."

"Anything juicy about this McTavish guy, David?"

"It's still a work in progress, but the man takes a lot of trips to Atlantic City, Las Vegas, and Monaco. So far he has a big bank account, but the sources of income to his accounts are not entirely clear. The sources of outgo are largely to casinos in those gambling cities. We're just getting started on Howard Marcus. I'll get back to you when we have more—like whether he's a high roller as well."

"Thanks," I tell him.

My pulse is beginning to quicken a little.

The next day in the staff meeting, Ivory reports that Howard Marcus is as jumpy as the proverbial cat on a hot tin roof.

"That brother is always lookin' over his shoulder, makin' sure I'm close by. Maybe he's been to too many cop and spy movies, but he regularly looks up at the tops of buildings—likely to see if there are any snipers. He has been workin' on his movie spycraft. If we walk outside, the man takes trips in the opposite way he's really headed, makes sudden turns, moves into crowds, and suddenly enters crowded department stores, and the like. He's not a talker—not a word of explanation about all of the anxiety."

The attentions of the staff are riveted on the security specialist's face. We all shake our heads, including Ivory.

"What have you got, Caitlin?" I ask her.

"Progress. Not electrifying, but progress. About two months ago, the Marcuses entered a stage where their outgo far exceeded their income until they were staring bankruptcy in the face. Then a miracle happened, as the antievolutionists like to say when things don't add up in the progression of things. The bank began a very rapid infusion of money to

Howard and Anne's personal account. The source is murky, and I mean very murky. In three weeks everything got to be hunky-dory, and it looks like they got to business as usual."

"How about young Decklin's accounts in all of this?"

"Funny thing. He does not seem to suffer or benefit from the all-American rags-to-riches story. In fact, he seems to have changed banks, gotten a new investment counselor, and put some distance between himself and his parents, at least financially. The neighbors report him coming to the house very frequently and that he appears to have a cordial social relationship with his parents right up to the time of his murder. Can't quite figure that out."

David Harger speaks up, "Carter Hinckley and I have spent the last nearly twenty-four hours with the NYPD forensic accountants. That combined our CPA's numbers expertise and my computer knowledge to augment the NYPD's. As an aside, we get along very well. Anyway, we served a warrant on the bank, and on both partners, Marcus and McTavish. We have been inundated with material—printed and electronic, verbal and telephonic, and have barely gotten started working our way into the mountain. A good thing about working with MacLeese and Redworth is that everything seems to be emanating from the police in the course of their investigation of Decklin Marcus's murder. I made myself small and obscure, and I don't think they are wise to the fact that I am a minion of McGee's.

"Something did come up. Do any of you recognize the name of Michael Soriano?"

"Give us a break," Caitlin says. "The better question is who doesn't know the name of Michael 'Pretty Boy' Soriano? He denies it in every criminal trial where he features prominently, but he is the boss-of-bosses of the Soriano family—murder, kidnapping, extortion, loan sharking, human trafficking, gambling, you name it."

"Yes, indeed; good detective memory, my friend Caitlin. I think you identified a couple of enterprises that may well be part of our murder mystery."

"It is premature," Caitlin continues, "but about two months ago—does that time-frame light any lights?—he began to make some truly remarkable investments in Global Investment Bank holdings. His big investments tapered off about the time both—and I underline *both*—Marcus and McTavish's fortunes once again began to rise."

"Great work, all of you," I tell them. "My gut and the little my brain has been soaking up tells me that we are on the right track. I have a suggestion along that line. Do a thorough electronic, paper, phone log search to see if a certain infamous Byelorussian gentleman figures in. For that matter, check the security check-in logs. Have MacLeese and Redworth get going on some in-depth interviews with bank staff—everyone from the janitors, mail-room guys, clerks, etc. all the way to the upper floors where the air is rarefied. Nobody needs to be altogether dainty about it, either. Somebody knows something we need to know. Let's pry it out of him or her. Okay, if there's nothing else, let's get out there and rattle some cages."

Chapter Seven

Detective First Grade Mary Margaret MacLeese and Detective Second Grade Martin Redworth are good at police work—knocking on doors, interviewing citizens and suspects, analyzing information to sort out the nuggets of truth from the mountains of baloney, and for getting people to unburden their souls by confessing. Working together for eleven years, they have developed a pattern of doing police work together that produces results. They both have commendations and decorations; they have both been injured in the line of duty; and neither of them retains the least vestige of illusion about the potential for evil in their fellow humans.

For six working days, they conduct interviews at New York's Global Investment Bank with the full endorsement of its president, Lincoln Vestor. The interviews are producing—if nothing else—a buzz of rumor among the staff. President Vestor follows the rumors with growing interest, beginning to realize that where there is smoke, there has to be some fire. He had heretofore avoided even the slightest idea that anything improper was going on in the bank's own investment unit—the fiefdom of

Howard Marcus and Reggie Whitehead. But now he is being forced to admit that he has been avoiding the warning signs because the bank's bottom line has never been healthier.

There are three executive assistants in the investments section. Interviews with two of them by Detectives MacLeese and Redworth have been unproductive of anything but a growing conviction that those two know something more than they are telling. Despite a day spent tag-teaming each of them, no solid leads develop. Today it is the turn of the newest addition to the investment unit's secretarial staff. Redworth is well aware of her past—a boyfriend with at least some ties to the Soriano crime family, and a more affluent lifestyle than her salary from the bank would permit.

"Hello, Ms. Martignetti," Redworth says in his calm, courteous manner. "Have a seat and relax. You seem pretty nervous. Take it easy. This is just routine. We have a few questions, and then you'll be on your way."

"Thank you, Detective. I am nervous. Would it be okay if you call me Oriana? It would be less formal, and I would be more at ease with your questions."

"Sure, and I'm Martin. Tell me a little about yourself. Like, where did you grow up, go to school, and how you got into banking? You have a pretty important position here in the bank; how did you get the job in investments?"

Oriana Martignetti is twenty-one years old, fresh out of CUNY with a bachelor's in finance, and has very little experience. Diego Clemente is her first serious boyfriend, and she is attracted to him because of his bad-boy flare. Redworth and MacLeese get all of that out of her in the first twenty minutes of their interview.

"What are your duties in the investment section, Oriana?" asks MacLeese.

"Well, if you really want to know the truth, I am just a glorified gopher. I get papers and reports ready for Mr. Whitehead. I make coffee, and I make sure he gets to his meetings on time. Sometimes I travel with him to Europe, and a few times I even went to Moscow with him to keep his arrangements and documents—that sort of thing—in order. It's pretty fun, but I kind of think it is a dead-end job. My education is better than that."

"I guess you have to start somewhere," Redworth observes.

"Yeah, but it's slow-going."

"You'd know 'slow' if you were a cop. It takes forever to get promoted or even to get noticed," MacLeese says.

"I guess I ought to be happy that I even have a job. More than half of my fellow business students who graduated with me last spring are still looking for a job."

"You must be something of a go-getter then. How'd you come to get this job? We had a look at your employment records. You were placed in the investment section right out of the starting gate, right?"

"I was lucky."

"I don't really believe in luck, Oriana. In this tough world, you have to have an edge. I hope you don't mind me saying so, but you are a classical Italian beauty. Maybe that helped. Or maybe you know somebody who knows somebody. What do you think?" asks Redworth.

"Don't tell anybody else, Detectives, but I guess I did sort of have an in."

"That sounds interesting. Tell us about it," MacLeese says.

"Promise you won't spread it around. The other girls would freeze me out if they knew that I have a sort of godfather."

"Ooh, that sounds interesting. C'mon, out with it," MacLeese leads the attractive girl to divulge her secrets.

"All right. This is the thing. My boyfriend—did I tell you about Diego?"

"I think you did. Go on."

"Well, he has some pretty interesting friends and an uncle who is big in the olive oil import business, I think it is. He's a nice man and a very good dresser. I tell you when he talks, people listen. I was almost scared of him at first, but he treats me like a favorite niece—a favorite Italian niece—which really counts for something."

"What's your 'uncle's' name, Oriana? He sounds like someone who's going to help you get up the ladder. You can never have too much of an in, you know," Redworth says.

"It's Vitaly Soriano. Diego says he's really well-connected. I think he's even friends of Mr. Whitehead. I don't know about Mr. Marcus, but Diego talks about his uncle and Mr. Whitehead belonging to the same Rotary club and going sailing together in the Caribbean—that kind of thing. Diego and me went on one of those trips. It was really fun."

"I'll bet it was. Now, Oriana, I really have to ask, do you talk to Diego or to Mr. Soriano about bank business? You know, just chit-chat sort of stuff?"

For all her naiveté and inexperience, and despite her very obvious physical charms, Oriana is not an airhead. Her antennae go up with that question.

"What do you mean?"

"Well, look, Oriana," MacLeese says, "I think you are perfectly aware of who Vitaly Soriano is. Isn't that right?"

"Maybe."

Redworth says, "Look, Oriana, you're a bright girl. You know that he's a big shot in one of the New York families. You are not dumb enough to be entirely taken in by that 'nice old uncle' stuff, right?"

"Yeah, I guess so. But Diego is a decent guy, and doesn't have a record or anything. Maybe he's kind of wild."

"I'm sorry, Oriana, but we're not buying the idea that you just happened to get this job. You are paid half again more than any of the other secretaries, did you know that?" MacLeese asks her, more pointedly now.

"I guess so. I guess that's right. What of it?"

"The 'what-of-it' is: what do you do for that extra money? How come you don't have to work all that hard, and you get to go on a bunch of nice trips? I think you're too smart to be sleeping with the boss. And I think you get more than a little extra money on the side from the Soriano family. Isn't that the long and short of it? And, for that, you pay back the nice uncle with a running account of what goes on in the investment unit. Isn't that right, too?"

Now, MacLeese's gloves are off, and Oriana realizes that she is in trouble.

"How do you know that?"

"We're detectives. It's what we do, Oriana," Redworth tells her.

"Am I in trouble?"

"Could be. But if you help us, maybe we can help you. Do you get what I'm trying to say to you? You're basically a good Catholic girl who might be getting in over your head. We want to help you, but you have to do something for us in return. Understand?" Redworth presses.

There is a pause while Oriana goes through the gamut of emotions and hurried decision making.

"I'm scared of the Sorianos. If they think I told you stuff about what I do for them, I could really get hurt. I just can't talk to you about that. I don't want to answer any more questions."

"Sorry, Oriana, but we know too much about you just to let it go. Talk to us. Give us everything, and we'll protect you. You can trust us," says MacLeese.

"If it gets that far, we could even get you into witness protection," Redworth tells her.

"Do I need a lawyer?"

"We don't know, do you?"

Another pregnant pause.

"If I get a lawyer, Diego and Uncle Vitaly will know. They seem to know everything. I do know stuff, but I have to be certain that I'll be protected; and I want immunity. I don't say anything more until I get written immunity. Okay?"

Detectives MacLeese and Redworth make two calls as soon as they finish Oriana Martignetti's interview. Oriana is taken to 1PP for her protection until the phone calls were completed.

MacLeese calls the chief of Ds.

"Chief, we have a break in the Decklin Marcus case."

"Let's hear it, Detective."

"We talked to a relatively low-level staffer at Global Investment Bank this morning. It happens that she is an Italian girl whose boyfriend is the nephew of Vitaly Soriano. The boyfriend is a low-level soldier in the Soriano family. The Sorianos have their fingers in Global's investments, especially in Europe. We think they probably hooked one of the major execs who got into debt, used a loan shark, couldn't pay, and traded his banking soul to pay off his debt. The girl has agreed to talk, but only if she gets immunity—written immunity—from a federal judge. I need your help."

"I've heard this refrain before, Detective. It's a familiar one—probably heard you sing it before. I'll get through to

Judge Davenport at the Second Circuit. He's understanding and quick. What's the witness's name?"

MacLeese tells him, and the wheels are set in motion.

Redworth calls McGee at his office.

"We caught a break. Actually two breaks. We have what appears to be a well-informed witness, an employee at Global Investment Bank. The other good thing is that we will have a letter granting immunity by two. Mary Margaret and I want to grill the girl's direct boss, and we think it would be a good idea for you to sit in. His name is Reggie Whitehead, and he is close to Howard Marcus and Angus McTavish."

"And you want to get him drained before you go for the vic's father, that about it?"

"In a nutshell."

"I'll be there."

"Is Caitlin up to speed on Whitehead's finances?" Redworth asks.

"We have a whole team dedicated just to Whitehead and Marcus. They will know everything there is to know by two o'clock today at the latest. We'll be ready. When and where do you want to meet?" I ask him.

"Tomorrow at ten—1PP, room 853."

"Got it."

MacLeese and Redworth walk down to the visitors' rooms on the third floor of the central police building. It is comforting to them to have to be searched no less than three times by experts. The security force rivals that of the sitting president.

They spend the next three hours getting the whole sordid story from Oriana. They record her confession that implicates the Sorianos and Reggie Whitehead in what looks to be a slam-dunk felony case. Then they head back to the bank.

Whitehead has heard the rumors and is visibly nervous—sweating and tugging at his collar. Caitlin and I purposely let him sit in the investment division conference room alone with nothing to do or read for an hour.

"Do you want some water? Coffee? Anything?" I ask when we enter the room.

"No."

If he thinks it is out of place for us two private eyes working in league with the cops to be offering him something from his own office kitchen, he does not show it.

"Well, then," I say, "we'll get started."

I take ten minutes to get all of the public data about himself from Whitehead, lulling him into a light torpor. Then I get to the heart of the conversation.

"Mr. Whitehead, do you know a woman named Oriana Martignetti?"

Whitehead's stony facial expression develops a crack—ever so tiny.

"Hmm…I think so," he reluctantly says, becoming instantly suspicious because he can tell where this was headed.

"Come now, Mr. Whitehead, you traveled to Europe, to Moscow, and took her to parties on your yacht. Isn't that true?"

"How did you know…?" he blurts, now fully aware that he is caught in a viselike trap.

I smile.

He frowns and sweats.

"Do I need a lawyer?"

"I don't know—do you? You know the old drill—you have the right to an attorney and all the rest of it. You can plead the Fifth Amendment to the Constitution of the United States not to incriminate yourself. In fact, you don't even have to listen to me, but I strongly advise you to do so. Financial chicanery may be unethical and hurt your career, or it may rise to the level of grand larceny and a prison sentence. The legal implications are beyond my legal training. However, that said, let me tell you this before you make your decision. Oriana Martignetti was the first to spill her guts to the NYPD detectives. She copped to her part in the entire crooked enterprise and even now is filling the DA in on details related to the murder of one Decklin Marcus. While we will only be too happy to see you go down for fraud, embezzlement and that sort of thing, what we came for is to get to the bottom of a murder. You are looking like the prime suspect in that crime. To be technical, the charge will be conspiracy to commit first degree murder for the purpose of stealing from your company, to silence a witness, and for the purpose of money laundering on a grand scale. You will go to prison for the rest of your life. I presume that the federal government will find a way to make RICO charges stick as well."

"You are probably overstating your evidence, Mr. McGee. But, hypothetically, what kind of a break could one in a position like you describe expect to gain from cooperating with the authorities?"

"That depends on how quickly you provide evidence—that is, if you beat the other likely suspects to the draw and how valuable your information is. Both the NYPD detectives and us private investigators take a dim view of murder. Decklin Marcus—so far as we can tell—was a decent young man with a great deal of promise who did not deserve to die. So, let me tell you this: if my partner and I leave this room without a serious promise and bring the NYPD into the room, your chances of getting a positive plea deal will become infinitesimally small."

Two things drive Reggie Whitehead at that moment. The first is that he is terrified of the American mafia and of another even worse threat. The second is the grim specter of the imposition of RICO statutes to his other potential sentences. He is no lawyer, but he has helped multiple clients evade the penalties under the Racketeer Influenced and Corrupt Organizations Act of 1970. He would end up forfeiting everything he owns, go away for life, and make his wife—the only decent part of his miserable life—destitute. More than anything else, that drives his decision.

He speaks quietly and considerably more humbly than when he first looked McGee and O'Brian in the eyes that afternoon.

"Will it hurt or help my case if I get a lawyer involved?" he asks.

I know I have him, "hurt, more likely than not," I say firmly, although I am not completely sure of my ground.

"I've heard about you, Mr. McGee. You have a pretty decent reputation as a straight shooter. I think I have about run out of options and am willing to talk to the police. I want you to be there when I do. I am about to make some terrible decisions; and I don't want to make them based on lies, all right?"

"I'll go out and give Detectives MacLeese and Redworth a call. My partner here will watch you while I'm gone. Don't make the slightest attempt to communicate with anyone outside this room. If you do, all plea deals will be off. We have yet to determine if you are low enough in the criminal hierarchy to be worth granting immunity. We clear on that, Whitehead?"

"Perfectly."

I call Mary Margaret and tell her what has transpired. She has been waiting in President Vestor's office trying to get a grip on how much he knows about what has been going on in his bank and how much he is a dupe. She is not satisfied that she has gotten what she needs yet.

Her cell phone plays the iconic song *Popular* from *Wicked*. The ID shows McGee's name and number.

"What do you have, McGee?"

"Another important link ready to cop a plea. You should come by the conference room and complete our chat with Whitehead. Bring Redworth, too. We will get farther faster if we gang up on this guy. He is in this up to his eyeballs."

"For the murder, too?"

"Probably not directly, but he at least has guilty knowledge with malice aforethought."

"I'm on my way."

She smiles at President Vestor and tells him that he needs to stay in the bank where she can find him for the rest of the day.

Chapter Eight

The two NYPD detectives walk briskly into the conference room to join me. Before she sits down, Mary
Margaret hands Whitehead a yellow lined legal pad and a
supply of pens. The effect is chilling in its presumptiveness.

"Now, Mr. Whitehead, Detective Redworth and I are very
busy. Don't waste our time."

"What do you want? What do you expect from me?"

"A full allocution. Nothing left out; nothing shaded
or exaggerated."

"Hey, wait a minute—I don't have a good basis for why I
should do any kind of confessing. What's the offer if I do?"

"We take the death penalty off the plate, for starters."

Whitehead winces and turns pale.

"That's all?" he asks.

"Depends on what you have to tell us."

"I could be killed if I mention anyone else who is involved.
I would have to have protection or be put in the FBI's Witness
Protection Program, at the least."

"If you are credible, we can whisk you off to Fort Meade where they are used to protecting important and endangered material witnesses awaiting their opportunity to testify against major targets. It is the ultimate safe house. After that, you might go to a federal penitentiary and be housed in protective custody. Or ... you might go into WitSec like you said. Depends."

"Before I say or write a thing, I have to know that RICO charges would be taken off the plate, too. I want my family left out of all of this. I don't really even know what RICO is all about, anyway."

Det. Redworth takes over for the moment, "The acronym RICO—I'm sure you know—is the Racketeer Influenced and Corrupt Organizations Act. Its main provisions include hefty fines—as much as double the gross profits or proceeds from the criminal gains—and prison sentences of twenty-to-life. You lose any interest and any present or future rights to any property involved in the racketeering enterprise and forfeit any ill-gotten gains that came out of the enterprise, including money or any property or objects of value. You will have to post a satisfactory performance bond. You can't transfer property to anyone to evade the penalties. Any property given to your wife or family resulting from the imposition of RICO penalties will be forfeited to the federal government. In very brief language—short of the death penalty—getting hung up by RICO is the ultimate bummer."

Whitehead seems to be shrinking before the eyes of the police and private detectives who are drilling holes in his eyes with theirs. There is no mercy in any of the four pairs of steely eyes staring into his.

"I'll cooperate all the way. Please put in a word about what I asked for. Please don't make it life in prison. I'm a family man. As soon as I complete writing down everything I know, you have to promise that you will get my family out of harm's way. They'll know in a minute. They always know, and they know everything, believe me."

"'They' being the Sorianos?" I ask for the record.

"Yes," he sighs.

He picks up the first pen and begins to concentrate on the yellow legal pad. Soon he is industriously filling page after page, pausing only to try to be accurate about dates, times, places, and people. What he produces will bring down the Soriano family and a significant number of Russian Mafiosos who are living in the US. He is also signing his own death warrant.

The detectives return in three hours to check on his progress. The legal pad and three pens are set aside, and the hard-nosed banker's head is lying on the conference table. He sits sobbing.

I sit beside him. "A couple of more things, Mr. Whitehead. First, did you kill Decklin Marcus?"

"Most certainly not!" he exclaims emphatically and convincingly.

"Did you order his death?"

"No, I didn't."

"Do you know who did?"

"Not for sure, and I would tell you if I did. I have my suspicions about the boy's father who had the most to lose if his boy ratted on us. Howard took the money from the Sorianos and the Russians as a lifeline just like I did. Both of us would be ruined if the truth got out. Angus McTavish was involved with the Sorianos just like Marcus and me, but I'm less sure of my suspicions about him for doing anything to harm Decklin than I am of Howard."

As soon as MacLeese and Redworth take Whitehead away to the safe house at Fort Meade, Caitlin, Ivory, and I put our heads together about what we should do next. Ivory—ever the up-the-center-charger—votes for a confrontation with Howard Marcus right now. Caitlin is an analyst, and she wants to learn more about Marcus's involvement with the Sorianos and what role the Russians played—are playing—in all of this. For the moment, we all agree that events have been moving so fast that it is likely that the Sorianos don't yet know what has come down.

"Okay," I say, "this is what I think we should do. Let's split up. Ivory, you're in pretty thick with the Marcuses. Why don't you have a slightly more than casual sit-down with them and see if they might accidentally spill a little. But not too much of Mr. Nice Guy. Before you leave them, you have to confiscate every means of communication to the outside of the house and get them isolated. Caitlin, get some of your old CIs to snoop and give us something that ties the family to either or both of the American or Russian mobs. Find Decklin's friends—use the NYPD's help, if you need to—and drag something out of them about a tie to the Russians. I am inclined to think that they are behind the killing; after all, one of their hit men did the deed. I am absolutely convinced that Mazurkiewicz did not act alone.

"I will get with the NYPD detectives and go to the FBI, the CIA, and Interpol to see if we can convince them to open a formal investigation in Russia. We have got to get hold of Viachaslau Mazurkiewicz, the Byelorussian wet work merc. That's probably the only way we can dig up anything on the Russian mob that will convince the Russian police to act. It may take a government to government intervention."

"A-a, boss, aren't you forgetting the little impediment that Homeland Security is obviously involved and highly unlikely to help? They may put the kibosh on our whole plan for reasons of their own," Ivory says.

"Yeah, I know," I say, "but I'm just going to blunder ahead and see what happens."

"Good plan," Ivory says. "You seem to have worked out all of the details."

I raise my one eyebrow in a withering look. He doesn't seem to wither.

My first call is to a friend from my time in the FBI, Darryl Strathmore.

"To what do I owe this honor, McGee?" he asks. "Oh, I think I can guess. You want something, and it is probably something you shouldn't have."

"I think I should have it," I say as lightly as I can under the circumstances.

"It's your nickel—shoot," he says.

I give Darryl better than a nickel's worth of explanation—more like the two-buck version—of what is happening in our case. He is patient.

"Tell me more about Homeland's involvement, McGee," he asks when I finish.

"I don't know more than what I told you. They came on like gangbusters and threatened to shut us down, but we haven't seen or heard anything more of them since."

"Don't be too sure that they're out of the picture. Everyone thinks the FBI is hard to deal with. They just haven't run crosswise with Homeland Security. Keep your guard up," Darryl says seriously.

"We are, and we will."

"Now, exactly what can I do for you?"

"We've got a lot of useful dirt on the key players at Global Investment Bank—enough to put some of them away for decades. We know who the actual murderer is, even though we probably don't have enough on him to extradite him or to get him into court yet. More importantly, we are sure that he works for much more important and much more secretive puppet masters; and we want them. What we need is for you to get a joint investigation into Viachaslau Mazurkiewicz with your counterparts in the Russian Ministry of Internal Affairs and get the police to pick him up and to hand him over to us."

"You know that's a tall order. Russian police have never been all that willing to cooperate with us, even in their own best interests. They are like the rest of the Russian agencies—secretive, dogmatic, arrogant, and very sensitive to slights. I'll get on it today. It happens to be a slow news day, and I need something interesting to do. But I can't make any promises."

"Your word that you will try is good enough for me, Darryl. Thanks."

My second call is blocked. So is my attempt at sending an encrypted e-mail. Our communications are all shut down tight. I know what comes next; so, I send Ivory and Caitlin out to do their work in person.

I am right. Less than ten minutes after I get them out the door, four large unsmiling men in dark suits, fresh white shirts, power ties, and shiny shoes walk into McGee and Associates Investigations with a search warrant and subpoena *duces tecum* in hand.

"I warned you," the older of the four agents says. "Now keep out of our way. Interfere, and you get an obstruction of justice charge and get to make an extended visit to Homeland Security offices here in New York or Washington, DC, or Elk Wallow, Idaho—whichever suits our fancy."

"Nice to see you again, Agent...?" I say with exaggerated politeness.

"It's Special Agent Hinckley, and you can skip the sugar. We're here on the business of national security. You're here to watch and keep out of the way of the real cops."

I show him my "much chastened" face and leave him to his search. Of course, since Hinckley's last search we have moved all of our sensitive records to our secret office in Vermont, and I am not worried. Having our communications jammed up is most inconvenient, however; and my next task of the day is to get them restored.

I walk to the outer office and saunter over to stand in the group of office workers to watch our government's finest security officers do their duty.

When the agents stop looking at me, I quietly turn aside to a low-level administrative assistant and whisper, "Nancy, here's a credit card. Go out and buy a box of burner phones and three voice distortion gadgets. Find Ivory and Caitlin and get those purchases to them. Don't be too obvious about it."

Nancy is happy to be a part of the solution. She walks to the ladies room where she spends five minutes then slips out the side door while the four agents and six forensic assistants rifle through our records, throwing papers all over the floor in an effort to create as much chaos as they can.

I walk up to Hinckley's side.

"Not to disturb you during your important government work, Special Agent Hinckley; but if there is something specific you want besides just scattering papers around, why not just ask me; and I can be of assistance. That would shorten your work day, and you nice government people can go out and have fresh doughnuts—or whatever—for the rest of the day and get credit for a full day's work. How about that?"

I think he wants to deck me, but he surprises me.

"Tell you what, McGee. We pretty much know what you have been up to and something of what you've found. I'll take you up on your offer. Box up all your records related to the Decklin Marcus case. Our people will come back tomorrow and pick them all up and include them into our files. Don't horse with me, McGee. Hold back and we'll be back with arrest warrants for you, your partners, and everybody who works for you. We've lost patience. Maybe this little exercise will convince you to leave the case alone. It is ours and ours alone."

"We'll get right on it," I say obediently.

Five minutes later the federal government vacates the premises, and I get the office personnel to work. Two secretaries gather up every paper off the floor and place them in their hopeless disarray into neat new unmarked manila folders. Carter Hinckley, our CPA, and Carolyn Zumbrowski, the chief administrative assistant, catch on quickly and get the troops to work. Two girls head off to buy boxes; Carter's assistant, Justin Rose, is sent to the attic store room with two of the secretaries who don't yet have an assignment to fetch down boxes of stored files. They prove to be very diligent workers. By four in the afternoon, they have three dollies which can carry four boxes each, and they each make ten trips. That is one hundred twenty boxes of files that date back as far as fifteen years ago—including old insurance forms, payroll records, business records related to trash collection, janitorial service, and rent, and a few outdated case records. The girls sent to get boxes are equally efficient and creative.

They gather their coworkers who mix and mingle file folders and their contents to ensure that no folder is accurately labeled, and no human being could ever rearrange the contents into a coherent record. We are absolutely in compliance with the law as demanded in the warrant and the subpoena duces tecum—"produce any and all records related to the above captioned case [the Decklin Marcus investigation]." Nothing in that document says anything about including boocoup additional material. After all, the subpoena did require delivery of "all records, documents, books, photographs, and electronic data." We are just trying to be fully compliant and helpful.

By six that evening, our resourceful—and now giddy—staff members have accumulated another seventy-two boxes—all unlabeled—of papers, some of which contain files labeled as "Decklin Marcus, suspicious death" case and some contain actual papers related to the case but not necessarily in accurately identified file folders. Although it has been a great deal of work, we include a letter absolving Homeland Security of any responsibility for creating an "undue burden or expense" that would entail sanctions on the federal government—just being good citizens. In addition—as required by the subpoena—we have included fifteen USB flash drives of electronic data, some of which relates to the case in question. The flash drives are in a clear baggie and are waiting near the back of the outer office for the officers who will want to remove all of the large boxes before getting to the baggie. There is a term for what we did in the technical language of attorneys: "Scattered tidbits of real mixed with mountains of "b—s—.""

Since the subpoena *duces tecum* does not include a command for appearance, I declare the following day to be an office holiday. The boxes are all neatly stacked and waiting for the government officers to collect. Admittedly the boxes so jam the limited space in the outer office that it could prove to be difficult for the large officers to navigate their way in, but we are confident in their level of ingenuity. We could have made all of this difficult for the federal agents by filing protests and requests for delays; or we could have found small irregularities in the language of the subpoena; but we thought that would not have been right. Therefore, relaxing our vigilance over our rights, we have complied--and with alacrity.

I, of course, do not hang around while my competent office staff does their work. I find Ivory and Caitlin and our newly purchased burner phones and voice distortion equipment, and we get to work.

Ivory arranges a meeting with the Marcuses for the same afternoon. Caitlin calls the NYPD detectives and brings them up to date on our recent dealings with Whitehead and our plans to interview the Marcuses again and invites them to join us. I put in a call to Langley to talk to Sybil Norcroft, the DCIA. This time, I use her top secret identifier code and get right through.

"McGee, this better be good," she says by way of greeting.

"And a fine day to you, as well, me fair lassie,"

"I'm not in the mood for Irish malarkey. What do you need this time?"

I know she's very busy; so, I give her the condensed version. She is very interested in the direction the case is taking, but her greatest interest lies in her innate distrust and disdain for Secretary Robert Carter, US Department of Homeland Security. If he is involved and interfering, there just might be something worth her agency's interest, especially if the

Russians are included in the web of secrecy the autocratic Homeland Security department is weaving.

"And you say that the NYPD detectives are working with your FBI agent friend to get the Russian police involved?"

"Yes."

"We might be able to help. Give me a couple of days, all right? Sounds interesting."

As soon as we complete that round of calls, Ivory, Caitlin, and I discard the burner phones we use. One of Ivory's men has taken a few burners around to the homes of our main staff people, and we do the business of the office via those phones for the next hour.

At two thirty in the afternoon, we all trek back to Gramercy Park where we meet Detectives MacLeese and Redworth and are let in through the locked gate. Anne Marcus and her maid meet us at the door to their house.

"Thank you for coming, detectives," she says. "You must have had some breakthroughs in the case. I certainly hope we are getting closer to catching whoever did this terrible thing to my boy."

Mrs. Marcus seems less down and better put together this afternoon in comparison to our previous meeting. I would have thought she might have heard something about our interviews with Oriana Martignetti and Reggie Whitehead, despite all of our efforts to keep a lid on the information. We take it as a good sign that we are going to have the advantage of surprise.

"Howard is in the library; we can meet in there."

The maid takes our coats, and we follow the lady of the house. Howard Marcus is standing in the center of the library waiting to welcome us, and glum as usual.

"Welcome. Make yourself comfortable. Can we get you anything before we start?"

"No thanks," we four detectives answer in an impromptu off-key chorus.

As per our agreement, Detective First, MacLeese, leads the conversation from our end. "I am going to address Mr. Marcus first, Mrs. Marcus. It is no slight to you and nothing sexist, but most of what we have to say involves him directly and not you, apparently."

Anne nods her understanding.

"I'll be blunt. NYPD and FBI forensic accountants have gone over your financials and those of your bank's with expertise and due diligence. To make a long story short, we learned that Reggie Whitehead—part of your investment unit at the bank—got into financial trouble, and you got involved in some failing financial schemes with him which were ruinous. You, Whitehead, and Angus McTavish got desperate and got linked up with Vitaly Soriano and his father, Michael "Pretty Boy" Soriano. He bailed you out, provided funds that made a substantial profit, and restored the three of you to power and wealth beyond what you imagined possible. It was a deal with the devil, Mr. Marcus. We have you dead to rights on charges of money laundering and of aiding and abetting an organized criminal group. We are not quite sure how the Russian mafia fits in, but they do. We will find that out after our international associates finish their investigation.

"We are certain that your son, Decklin, got wind of your criminal activities, moved all of his holdings to another bank, put some physical distance between you and him, and was probably in the process of informing NYPD and the FBI, and maybe the security division of the American Bankers Association, and the SEC."

Marcus turns deathly pale. His left eyelid goes into involuntary spasms.

"Mr. Marcus, you are under arrest for participating with racketeers to launder money and to defraud your bank, for embezzlement, and for suspicion of murder. You have the right to remain silent. If you give up that right, anything you say can and will be used against you in a court of law. You have the right to an attorney and to have that attorney present during questioning. If you cannot afford an attorney, one will be provided for you at no cost. Please stand up."

He stands up, and Martin Redworth puts him in handcuffs. His face becomes as blank as a cheap haberdashery mannequin.

"Is that absolutely necessary? I don't believe for a second that my husband did any of that—most certainly he did not kill our son. That is unthinkable!" Mrs. Marcus blurts out.

She weeps uncontrollably now. The hearts of all the detectives go out to her, but as I had promised on the first day I met Howard Marcus, I would let the chips fall where they may.

"Is a deal possible?" Howard asks.

Det. MacLeese is angry, and her response is cold, "No."

We are not certain how he learned about our coming for him, but Angus McTavish evidently got advance warning. I suspect Anne Marcus, but who knows? When we get to the McTavish house in Boerum Hill neighborhood of Brooklyn—one of the ten most expensive and exclusive neighborhoods in any of the five boroughs—we find a distraught wife who has to be supported to stand by her son and a Latina maid. They lead us to McTavish's home office where he is hanging from a rope attached to the chandelier. His antique colonial chair is lying on its side on the parquet floor. There is no question about his being dead.

Det. Redworth picks up a blank envelope from McTavish's desktop. Inside, on cream-colored heavy bond letterhead paper is a simple declaration: "I'm terribly sorry more than you can even imagine. I am a thief. I have failed myself, my bank, my clients, my family, and my friends. I cannot face the consequences. I am a coward. Try to forgive me someday." It is signed "A.M."

There is no mention of murder or of Decklin Marcus, and no confession with enough detail to be useful in court. We can only consider his suicide one more dreadful piece of fallout from this set of interwoven crimes. It is sad—but not unjust—we all reflect.

On the way back to NYPD, MacLeese gets a call on her cell phone. She listens briefly, says "Thanks," and puts her iPhone back in her purse.

"Anything?" I ask.

"Yeah," she says. "That was the desk sergeant at Robbery-Homicide. Seems that agents from Homeland Security will be meeting Redworth and me when we get back to 1PP."

"Lucky you," I say. "We'd better get a cab and make ourselves scarce. Here's a throwaway cell; use it to call me on my burner when you get away from the feds. The number is downloaded to your new phone."

"Okay," she says, not feeling altogether perky.

Chapter Nine

Things are worse than MacLeese and Redworth envision during their ride to One Police Plaza. Sergeant Greene escorts them to the chief of D's office. He is not alone, not by a long shot. Sitting in a democratic circle of chairs are: besides Robert Wainwright, the chief of detectives; Trayhorn Jones, the new NYPD commissioner of police; New York SAC, Douglas Merkley, special agent, FBI, Darryl Strathmore, special agent, Homeland Security, Dwight Hinckley; and Maxwell D. Bond, special assistant to the mayor of New York. It is a daunting sight for the two NYPD homicide detectives.

"Have a seat, Detectives," Chief Wainwright says. "Let's get started. Commissioner Jones asked for this meeting to clear the air."

The commissioner says, "My office gets two or three complaints a week from Homeland Security about one of your cases, Detectives. They insist that they ordered you to cease and desist your involvement, and you have not complied. Why is that?"

"Because we caught the case—a murder in the city of New York. As far as we can tell, Homeland Security doesn't care a whit about the murder of our victim, Decklin Marcus. We do; and we have uncovered a conspiracy that definitely involves the Soriano crime family, three executives of Global Investment Bank, and maybe involves the Russian mafia," Det. MacLeese says matter-of-factly—a demonstration of defiance to Dwight Hinckley's way of thinking.

"What part in all of this does Homeland Security play, Special Agent Hinckley?" the commissioner asks, turning to the federal agent.

"That's classified," he replies without looking at the commissioner.

"How does the murder of a citizen of the city of New York figure into a classified federal interest?"

"That's classified," Hinckley says, now looking diffidently at the commissioner.

"I think it is time to abbreviate this meeting," Commissioner Jones says. "Is your answer to every question any of us ask you here today going to be 'that's classified'?"

"Pretty much. But I will add the other pertinent reason for me being here: you will remove your uncooperative detectives and your department from the Decklin Marcus case. You will stand down."

New York City Commissioner of Police Trayhorn Jones is a black man who has spent a career hearing federal agents *telling* him to back off cases. He did not like any of that when he was a patrolman, and he likes it even less now.

"Take this back to your boss, Secretary Robert Carter, US Department of Homeland Security," Jones says. "The death of Decklin Marcus is entirely within the purview of the NYPD's jurisdiction and responsibility. These two fine detectives have my full support and that of the entire NYPD. Their investigation will continue to its logical conclusion, and we will not allow interference by you or anyone else. Let me put it more clearly: if you interfere, you will be charged with obstruction of justice. You can go impress someone else with your 'it's classified' BS"

"We'll see about that," Hinckley says and stands up to leave.

"Indeed we will, Special Agent. Until and unless the president of the United States himself gives us an order, we will not back away."

"That can be arranged, Commissioner," Hinckley said as he walks out of the door.

"That went well," says Max Bond, the mayor's representative. "However, this time I think the mayor will support you. He is sick and tired of the feds riding roughshod over the city, and looks at this Decklin Marcus affair as a test case."

When the meeting breaks up, both FBI Special Agent Strathmore and Mary Margaret MacLeese call me and give me a blow-by-blow. I put in a call to Sybil Norcroft and let her know that the case is getting even weirder. She says it is "stimulating"—which I find a bit strange—but she seems pretty calm about it; so, I decide not to worry overmuch.

The idea of not "worrying overmuch" may have been premature, I decide, when—the next day—I get a summons to meet the president of the United States in the Oval Office. His secretary tells me that we will be discussing the Decklin Marcus case, and that the DCIA and the secretary of Homeland Security will be in attendance. That sounds like very heavy stuff, but I signed up to see the whole case to the end. So I guess it's a matter of "if you're in for a penny, you might as well be in for a pound."

Chapter Ten

I like the way President Willets does things. He's a man after my own heart, and it appears that DCIA Norcroft is of the same mind. President Willets meets us at the door to the Oval Office and has us sit in a semicircle of comfortable chairs and small couches facing the Lincoln desk. Everyone arrives at about the same time. "Everyone" includes the secretary of State, the secretary of Homeland Security, NYPD commissioner of police, the DFBI, the DCIA, and four little people. I am one of those little people; the other three are Detectives MacLeese and Redworth, and Special Agent Hinckley. The mood is decidedly negative with the federals looking daggers at us locals, and vice versa, with the exception of me. I am the picture of placid acceptance of being in the epicenter of this potential battle between the titans.

If that were really true, why do I feel like this is going to be one of those situations that the old African proverb describes, "When the elephants fight, what gets hurt is the grass?" In truth I am on tenterhooks wondering what twist of fate has brought me into this fight between elephants.

"Thank you all for coming, ladies and gentlemen. We are all very busy people; so, I won't waste time with chatting. Secretary Carter and Commissioner Jones have briefed me about what is basically going on here. Let me state that what is said here, stays here, when we leave here. Anybody have an objection to that?"

Everyone in the room nods in acceptance of that executive order.

"First, let's hear from Secretary Carter."

"I am here because the president ordered me to be; and further, he ordered that I divulge highly classified information. I am reluctant to do so, but hopefully everyone here is a patriotic American and will honor the president's order to maintain secrecy."

His disdain for the rest of us is almost palpable.

"Not to burden you with too many details, this is what Homeland knows: there is a complex interrelationship among elements of the main branch of the *russkaya mafiya* called the *Solntsevskaya Bratva;* the New York crime syndicate, the Soriano family; executives of the Global Investment Bank's bank investment unit; the Howard Marcus family; and particularly, the murder victim, Decklin Marcus. One of the bank's investment unit's executives, Reggie Whitehead, gets himself and his partner Howard Marcus into dangerous financial trouble by investing with none other than Bernard Lawrence Madoff who is currently—and for the next 150 years to come—residing in the Butner Medium Federal Correctional Institution outside Butner, North Carolina, near Raleigh.

"Enter the Sorianos. Whitehead makes a pact with the devil and arranges a bailout with loan sharks controlled by Michael "Pretty Boy" Soriano and his nephew, Vitaly. Since Howard

Marcus and another bank executive named Angus McTavish colluded with Whitehead to use bank money to invest with Madoff, they were also desperate enough to go along with Whitehead's deal. In brief, the deal is to look the other way when the Sorianos deposit huge sums of undocumented cash into the investment unit's accounts—money laundering pure and simple, and on a staggering scale. Not only do the bank executives avoid the humiliation and possible criminal charges stemming from their misappropriation of bank funds, but they become billionaires several times over.

"This illegal activity might have gone unnoticed had Decklin Marcus—son of Howard Marcus—not become aware of his father's involvement. The young man was a moralist and a purist of the first order and became completely estranged from his father. He knew his father's logins and passwords and used that information to get into his father's and the bank's secret account sites. He made a thumb drive copy of all of the incriminating data then left the family home for an apartment somewhere in the Bronx. He transferred all of his personal funds—which were substantial on his own—to another banking firm. He then pressured his father to come clean. Mr. Marcus told Whitehead what his son was doing, and Whitehead told Vitaly Soriano. The rest is somewhat conjecture, but we think young Decklin was then murdered by an operative hired by the *Solntsevskaya Bratva*. To put a cap on it, Angus McTavish kills himself and leaves a suicide note."

"What has this to do with Homeland Security? Sounds like a case of murder-for-hire by mobsters in New York," asked Commissioner Jones.

"I haven't finished, Commissioner. Homeland Security is alerted when it comes to our attention that the source of most of the Soriano's ill-gotten gains is from the sale of heroin. The source of that heroin is from Golden Triangle opium poppy plantations under the control of al-Qaeda. The heroin is transported by the Soriano family's connections with Russian mob protection in a complicated deal where profits are split between the crime family, the Russians, and al-Qaeda. The funds were funneled from the Sorianos through the bank and then to legitimate businesses established by the American crime syndicate, to similar Russian mafia businesses, and about half going to an assortment of phony Islamic charities controlled almost entirely by al-Qaeda—the most notable of which is the Universal Islamic Assistance Foundation headed by Usama ibn al Bakr. The charities use a pittance to support their legitimate humanitarian functions and to build Islamic schools called Madrasahs. The majority of the money goes to jihadists who perpetrate terrorist attacks throughout the Middle East, Europe, and some in the US. Universal Islamic Assistance Foundation is given $286 million, of which only $10 million could be accounted for as having been received by legitimately needy individuals and organizations. Aware of much of the linkages, Decklin Marcus went to the FBI for starters, but he thought it would be better handled by Homeland Security. That is how we became involved."

President Willets asked Commissioner Jones to comment.

"Mr. President, most of this is new to me and to my detectives. The way I now see it is that there can be a good working relationship between NYPD and the federal government agencies. We have already found—with some federal help— that Decklin was murdered by the use of a very sophisticated poison supplied by the Russian *mafiya*. We have evidence we think is probably enough to indict and to convict an operative of the Russians—a Byelorussian mercenary hit man named Viachaslau Mazurkiewicz—whose present where-abouts are unknown. We have arrested the primary perpe-trators of the financial crimes, including the murder victim's own father and the principal Soriano crime family members. We are anticipating a domino effect of small fry escaping punishment by implicating their bosses. It is a work in prog-ress. Howard Marcus is being held without bail for the time being as a co-conspirator in the death of his son, but I have to admit that the evidence is a bit shaky on that score. As I see it, our NYPD detectives should continue to work the narrow issue of Decklin's murder, and Homeland Security should continue to work the terrorism angle."

"And I think your NYPD is in over its head. Not only do you not have an adequate idea of the complexity of what is going on in this case—of which the murder is only a small part—but you do not have either the resources or the authority to pursue the international and terrorism aspects of it. This is a Homeland Security issue, and that's final," says the steely-eyed secretary of Homeland Security.

Commissioner Jones starts to speak, but the president cuts him off.

"Hang on a minute, Commissioner. I think it is time for us to hear from the CIA as a matter of practicality," President Willets says, holding up his hand as a stop sign.

Jones nods.

DCIA Sybil Norcroft turns her chair around; so, she can face the men in the room directly.

"Thank you, Mr. President. I think the CIA can make a definite contribution. As I see it, one of the linchpins in this entire case is the Byelorussian hit man. We have the resources to locate him, and hopefully, to bring him in. We can work with our counterparts in Russian intelligence to find him.

He can even be interrogated in the Russian system, which—I don't need to emphasize—has a more vigorous attitude toward interrogation than we do. I know that because I have already been in communication with Colonel General Yevgeni Mitrokhin, Director of the SVR [Foreign Intelligence Service] and Michael Levinovich Ledvinov, Director of the MVD [Ministry of Internal Affairs] who are only too happy to help and thereby to avoid an international incident that might link their government with the *Solntsevskaya Bratva*, Islamic terrorists—a mutual enemy of ours and theirs—and international drug traffickers—a current and continuing concern for the Russian government. In my opinion, we need to wrap the entire case up into one final neat bundle. We can only do that by utilizing all of our resources and by cooperating with each other. Turf battles should be set aside."

Secretary Carter and Special Agent Hinckley glare openly at Dr. Norcroft, but think it wiser not to speak for the moment. It is now up to the president.

President Willets temples his fingers on his forehead and has a moment of quiet thought and decision making.

"There has been a great deal of friction and chest beating over this case. It is too important to lose more time in silly and unproductive marking of territory and in internecine squabbling. So, this is what we are going to do: I will have a presidential order drawn up. You will all take a breath, step back, and begin anew. In the new world we will create, everybody will cooperate fully; everyone will speak and otherwise communicate with civility; and, above all, every bit of information will be shared. You will meet regularly—weekly, if not daily—to keep everyone posted. Beginning today, CIA will handle the foreign aspects. Homeland will deal with the jihadists and their confederates in this country. NYPD will work in their own way to bring the murder conspirators to justice in New York.

"As more than an aside, I hereby order Homeland Security to cease and desist with its campaign of harassment and interference with the activities of McGee & Associates Investigations. Their records will be returned in good order and promptly—as in the next forty-eight hours. I will tell you that Mr. McGee has been instrumental in the past to solve a very vexing problem for us. We want him to be included. Any questions?"

I certainly have none. I have to restrain myself from jumping up and down; my NYPD detective friends make an effort not to present a self-satisfied smirk; and Commissioner Jones and Secretary Carter avoid eye contact with each other. The minor cogs like myself and my detective friends quietly make plans to have a little celebration lunch; and no doubt, the Homeland Security officials are planning a different kind of lunch—heaping plates of crow.

Chapter Eleven

D avid Harger, head of IT, asks me for a meeting.
"What's up, David?"

"I'm not quite sure, boss; but I have some research stuff from the Marcuses you ought to look at."

He shows me some rather disjointed printouts with a mixture of complete and partial messages and a lot of gibberish that he tells me is the encrypted material.

"These are e-mail logs resurrected from the 'delete' files. That's why they look so poorly organized. Most of them come from what we were able to extract from both the Marcus computers. I had to work with the IT department of NYPD to get Howard's materials since his computer has been impounded. There's not a lot there that would surprise you; and nothing that links him to his son's murder. Not that it is our primary concern, but I have copies of several hundred documents which link him to the Sorianos; so, he's toast on the criminal money laundering charges. It practically took an act of Congress to get the records that Homeland Security sequestered. Quite a bit of that has been redacted—so much for interagency cooperation. What I do have is conspicuous for its absence of any communications with the al-Qaeda sources.

"The material from Whitehead, McTavish, Oriana Martignetti, and both Sorianos does include encoded communications with a guy named Umar al Sharif who is a known affiliate of a major Taliban cell based in Peshawar and an al-Qaeda cell operating in Al-Awja, Iraq—the birthplace of Saddam Hussein—and a larger town, Tikrit. The Homeland Security people were able to break the encryption code—it is a book code based on the Hadith—and that ties the bank investment unit to the Sorianos and a guy named Muhammad Hassan al-Begat, who seems to be the go-between for the Al-Awja cell, the Russian and American Mafiosos, and the Marcuses, and the other bank execs. We have some printouts that serve more or less as the Rosetta Stones of the case."

"That still doesn't get us the clear link to anybody in the conspiracy to murder Decklin, though, right?" I ask.

"Not exactly," David responds, "but there is something very interesting—new, actually—in a couple of the e-mail logs that Homeland decrypted. Look."

I am holding a printout that reads:

"I have the info on Achmed and the directions to move the necessary packages through the *hawala* people. I will see that the packages are in the warehouse. The contents are untraceable, of course. Now, you need to finish the arrangements with your agent, V.M."

"I've heard of *hawala*, but I'm not sure I know exactly what it is," I tell him.

"*Hawala* is the informal money transfer system used in the Middle East and often by jihadist terrorist organizations to move money without formal records. It is often friend-to-friend or family member-to-family member, and is based on the complicated mix of performance and honor of a huge network of money brokers. Apparently, there is almost never a breach of security or any theft. It just isn't done. Even if *hawala* is the suspected method of transmittal of funds, it is all but impossible to produce tangible proof."

"So, the question of the day is: who authored the e-mail?"

David says, "It's not signed, of course, but it came from Mrs. Marcus's computer."

"And, am I to presume that 'V. M.' is our own Viachaslau Mazurkiewicz?" I ask.

"Not for certain, but presumably," he answers.

The implications are almost too much to take in, and I have to make my mind work on all sorts of possibilities before I can finally accept what seems to be obvious.

I get a call on my iPhone from Sybil Norcroft.

"Hello, McGee, how're things going today?"

"Pretty well. We have some e-mail log files that nail the Sorianos and the executives of the bank investment unit at Global Investment Bank. That is a package, and NYPD is wrapping up the evidence for trial. That will take a while because there is so much data to sift through. The most interesting thing from my point of view is that there is some suggestion that Anne Marcus—our victim's mother—is somehow involved. That is a bit tenuous at the moment."

"I called because I have some news, as well," the DCIA says.

"Okay, hit me with it," I tell her.

"Company people may have located Viachaslau Mazurkiewicz we think."

"Is he in custody?"

"Not just yet."

"Where is he?"

"As of two hours ago, he is in an apartment on Han Asparuh Street in Varna, Bulgaria. In case you aren't all that familiar with Bulgaria, Varna is located on the west coast of the Black Sea near the Stone Forest. The Russian mafia moved him there under the protection of the tlM—the Bulgarian mafia, for lack of a better term. They are protected by the Bulgarian Secret Service, a through-and-through corrupt governmental agency. We cannot expect any help from official quarters."

"Swell," I say. "So what do we do?"

"Two of my best people are watching the apartment as we speak. I have ordered a rapid response team to gather in Varna. They should be there in a day. I have to attend to some Company business in Moscow later in the week; so, I plan to take a small detour and go to Varna myself."

"In disguise, I hope."

"Of course. We have the best Hollywood makeup artists there are at our beck and call."

"Any chance of my guy, Ivory White, and I going along?"

"Is he the black guy I've heard about?"

"The same."

"Actually, his race may prove to be a good cover. Is he as good at field work as I hear?"

"Better."

"Are you up for a little adventure yourself, McGee?"

"Yes, Ma'am. You couldn't keep me away."

"All right, come by my office at four this afternoon. This is not for communication on an insecure phone. I will lay out the plan then. Bring a toothbrush."

As soon as I hang up, I get hold of Ivory and Caitlin for a meeting in my office.

"Hey, Ivory, how would you like to take a little adventure tour of Bulgaria?"

"Sure," he says. "Do I have to pack anything special?"

"Your best stuff."

He nods his understanding.

"When do we leave?"

"This afternoon?"

"How about me, boss?" Caitlin asks.

"You have something more pressing to do. I want you to sift through every paper that David, the NYPD, and Homeland Security has on Anne Marcus. The thick looks like it's beginning to plotten there. I doubt that Ivory and I will be all that long on our trip, and I would like to have a serious and well-planned talk with the matriarch of the Marcus family when we get back."

"Will do," she says. "Do I presume that your trip is not to be broadcast abroad? Maybe includes a puzzle palace involvement?"

"Maybe so," I answer, and flash her one of my patented enigmatic smiles.

She and Ivory laugh.

CIA Special Agents Mac Young and Ed Simonsen are sitting in a small outdoor café on Varna's Sveti Kliment Street near its intersection with Han Asparuh Street. They have a well-shaded table in a nondescript internet café with a good view of the Armenian Church, Plaza Ekzarh Jossif, and the Draguz Apartment building on Han Asparuh. For the past two mornings they have unobtrusively scoped out the streets for evasion and escape routes, and are satisfied that they are in as good a location as any to prepare for their assault. They have been there all this morning. Mazurkiewicz was seen entering the building at two in the morning after a heavy drinking party at a secret service general's house near the Sea Gardens on very upscale Bulevard Primorski. The area was quiet all night and is still just beginning to wake up this morning. The only people that Mac and Ed take note of are four obvious security agents—burly thugs—who make hourly patrols around the block where the Draguz Apartment building sits. The two agents presume that the men are secret service. The bulges in their ill-fitting jackets suggest strongly that they are well armed.

Sybil, two seasoned female, and two male agents from covert-ops at Langley, McGee, and Ivory, arrive in two cheap nonmetered cabs they got from the cabstand at the airport. The cabs are old Soviet vintage sedans, battered and of questionable reliability. A tourist would be very hesitant to get into such a taxi and with good reason. However, Ivory's presence makes the idea of robbery, mayhem, kidnapping, or murder less enticing in the minds of the drivers and their associates from tlM. Sybil is an old hand at haggling, and the two taxis are hired for a ridiculously cheap fare.

They get out in front of the Armenian Church and saunter in the direction of the internet café where Mac and Ed are sitting and separately find empty tables for themselves. They order plates of Sirene and Kashkaval [salty white cheese and cow's milk cheese, respectively], a selection of banitsa pastries, moussaka, and bowls of tarator [cold yogurt and cucumber soup]. The food is restorative after the long flight and bumpy cab ride.

Ed gets up and heads toward the restrooms. Sybil waits a few minutes then excuses herself and leaves in the direction of the lady's room. She and Ed meet in the backyard of the café amidst the sights and smells of cooking, garbage, and the sounds of pigs being slaughtered the old-fashioned way.

"How does it look, Ed?" Sybil asks, getting right to the point.

"So far so good, boss. He went into the building late last night and hasn't been seen since. We have a woman posing as a cleaning lady who is keeping an eye on his apartment. As far as she can tell, he has stayed in his rooms all night."

"Which floor?"

"Fifth."

"Guards?"

"Four. They are almost certainly secret service; so, they are not as dumb as they look. And anything they lack in brains, they make up in brawn. Those guys were probably brought in from the farm where they used to eat hay and pull a plow. They are huge and maintain a rigid no-nonsense schedule. The good news is that they have a highly predictable schedule, night and day."

He looks at his watch.

"They will be walking past each other in front of the apartment building in a couple of minutes."

"Where can we take them out?" Sybil asks pragmatically, with no more sympathy than if she were discussing the fly problem in the café.

"The backyard is perfect. It's full of junk. No self-respecting person would venture anywhere near there in the dark. If the sharp-edged trash doesn't get you, then the things that go bump in the night will. We can slip in there with night vision goggles one at a time and set up an ambush. The guards do drink and won't be at their best by around three."

"Sounds like a plan. We can't sit around in the café all day. What can we do with ourselves?"

"We have a room in a flophouse on Knyaz Boris. It's a rundown section within walking distance. Nobody pays any attention to anybody else over there. It is one of the few laws the people who live there obey. All of our stuff is in the room. We have some lunch meat, cheese, and Pirinsko beer. It's all pretty good, and keeps us going."

"Sounds good. We'd better split up over the next twenty or thirty minutes and get to the room. We can each take turns watching Mazurkiewicz's apartment building," Sybil says, having some difficulty pronouncing Mazurkiewicz's name.

"Easy for you to say," Ed laughs.

Sybil crinkles her nose at him, and they split up and return to their tables.

The team holes up in their rooms until late evening. Their quarry has not been out all day. A woman visits him during the late afternoon and leaves at seven. Otherwise, there is no evident activity on the part of Mazurkiewicz. The team holds a meeting and determines a plan, selects and sets aside the equipment they presume they will need, and pours over a detailed city map to be doubly sure of their escape route. A baking company van will be just around the corner from the apartment building ready to cover the extraction.

Everyone is bored stiff and hungry for something more exciting than lunch meat and yogurt. Mac has reconnoitered a café that looks to be reasonably safe; so, they take a small risk and walk in pairs and at separate times to get something to eat. The traditional Bulgarian grill—*Skara-tatarsko kufte—shishcheta* [shish kabobs], *karnache* [sausage with spices]—*sarma* from the main entrée menu, and dessert baklava are excellent and sits well on their empty stomachs. The food buoys them up. They are ready for action when they leave the café at midnight. It is a long and boring three-hour wait before they can go into action.

Mac and Ivory make one last scouting trip at two-thirty and report back to the team that everything is still quiet. Another woman has come and gone between midnight and one thirty, but Mazurkiewicz is presumably sound asleep when Mac and Ivory leave the vicinity of the apartment building. Everything looks to be safe.

"Okay," Sybil orders, "one at a time. See you in the backyard."

The men and women carry fairly heavy backpacks. One male and one female agent and McGee are selected to be sentries for the team. The rest—Sybil, Mac, Ed, and Ivory, along with three covert ops agents—make their way through the shadowy streets and pick their way into the areas of larger pieces of trash in the backyard of the seedy apartment building.

The team determines two escape routes and silently sets up three ambush sites. Sybil checks everything four times before she is satisfied. They work even as the security guards make their rounds, stopping only when the guards get too close. Sybil and her CIA team, McGee and Ivory, are ready.

Chapter Twelve

C aitlin and her two assistants, and David Harger and his
  senior technical assistant, put in ten-hour days gathering
anything and everything ever written or photographed by or
about Anne Marcus. It is largely an exercise in tedium, but
the occasional nugget pops out of the sluice. Taken in aggre-
gate, the nuggets are becoming a growing gold bar of useful
information. Caitlin looks in the *New York Times* archives
and finds nothing until she decides—on a whim—to go
through a couple of decades of the social column. In 2011,
there is a large picture of the executive staff of the Global
Investment Bank at a fund-raising gala for charity. That is
not in and of itself remarkable, but—as the saying goes—the
devil is in the details. The name of the charity rings a bell
for Caitlin. It is Universal Islamic Assistance Foundation.
Receiving an enthusiastic hug is Usama ibn al Bakr, the foundation's president. The woman hugging him is Anne Marcus.
It is a very clear color photograph. The reporter commented
on Mrs. Marcus's perfect choice of an evening gown by Vera
Wong for the occasion, and the magnificence of her diamond

jewelry. Mrs. Marcus is quoted in the article describing al Bakr, as "my dear friend."

The only other photograph shows the executives of the Global Investment Bank's internal banking investment group and their wives at a retreat at the Four Seasons Hotel on Nevis Island in the Caribbean, the most successful off-shore banking system in the Caribbean—more secure for American investors seeking anonymity from the IRS, the FBI, private creditors, and divorce attorney forensic accountants than the Cayman Islands. It cannot be a coincidence that Usama ibn al Bakr is standing next to Anne Marcus in an apparent tête-à-tête.

David and his forensic accountants bring up several nuggets of their own. They produce four receipts signed by Mrs. Marcus at the Four Seasons, and—also not a likely coincidence—they find four receipts at the same hotel for ibn Bakr. Although not related directly to ibn Bakr or to the bank, there are multiple hotel receipts from around the world that appear to indicate that attractive Mrs. Marcus does a considerable amount of traveling without her husband. It is evident that the socialite has an active social life without her family. One final nugget is concrete evidence that both the Marcuses and the Sorianos have accounts in Nevis banks; and, more importantly, that Anne has an account under her own name in addition to the joint accounts. The forensic accounting equivalent of a *coup de grâce* comes in the form of the discovery of a heretofore unreported account at the main branch of the Bank of America in San Francisco under Mrs. Marcus's maiden name—Warren. The account yields a complex financial history with the bottom line being holdings of $350 million. There is no reasonable accountancy for the source of such a vast sum. McGee's forensic accountants are not so designated for light and transient reasons.

Caitlin and her assistant, Rosalie Hertel, take a set of glossies around the area of Decklin's apartment in the South Bronx. The apartment itself is still marked off with yellow crime-scene tape. The photographs are of Anne Marcus; they were freely given to Caitlin and McGee on their first visit to the Marcus's Gramercy Place home. The other set of photos are of Usama ibn al Bakr of Universal Islamic Assistance Foundation fame scanned from the front cover of the foundation's brochure without proper attribution. This is real flat-foot cop work—the kind of work that earns beat cops the dubiously complimentary nickname. After knocking on more than 300 doors and showing the photographs to more than a thousand people, Caitlin and Rosalie come up with a large and valuable nugget—positive IDs for both individuals shown in the photos. By the third day, they have collected eleven non-addict, non-crazy, English-speaking witnesses, willing to testify that they had seen the two people individually—and in four instances, together—during the past year. A piece of pure gold comes from a salesman who lives in an apartment half a block away from Decklin's. He describes seeing the attractive upper-crust woman New Yorker and a "swarthy Arab" looking at and pointing toward the fire escape on the side of Decklin's building. Rosalie makes a record of everyone who recognizes either of the two people in the photos and gets all of the demographic particulars. She and Caitlin consider that they have done a fine three days of work and deserve a glass of white wine on the firm's dime.

Caitlin and Rosalie take their investigation a big step further—which in retrospect may turn out to have been a big mistake. They wangle permission to see Mrs. Marcus herself using the good offices of FBI Special Agent Darryl Strathmore, longtime friend of McGee's. She is being protected in a super-secure area of Fort Meade, Maryland, set aside to protect important VIPs and witnesses—usually those whose lives are in jeopardy from being involved in mob trials.

Anne Marcus is genuinely glad to see them—to see anyone. Her stay is a lonely one because her visitors are almost entirely limited to cops, FBI agents, and attorneys. It is a welcome diversion to get to talk to a couple of attractive and well-dressed women not much younger than herself. Although they are detectives, they are not cops in the same way as her usual keepers; and she considers that a plus.

"Thanks from coming clear out here to see me. It is just mean that I can't use the phone or the computer to communicate," Mrs. Marcus says as soon as the women sit facing each other."

"Thank you for having us on such short notice," Caitlin says.

They have a short period of girl talk; but it is strained, because it is obvious that Caitlin and Rosalie are there on business.

Finally, Anne tires of the stilted conversation and plunges in, "So, Caitlin and Rosalie, what business brings you here? Do you have a better handle on my son's killer?"

"It is beginning to look like we do. We'll bring you up-to-date after we ask you a few questions. That okay with you?"

"Sure."

Caitlin takes out her notebook and reviews it before starting her questions.

"Would you please tell us about your education? Maybe something about your math and accounting experience?"

Caitlin and Rosalie already know everything there is to know about Anne Warren Marcus's education. This first question is just a softball designed to see if Anne is going to tell the truth. She passes. She has had a fine education. Her parents presumed that she would marry well and saw to it that she could use her good head for numbers. Before she went to Bryn Mawr College in Pennsylvania, they made her take a year of accounting and statistics. She was only too happy to share that with the private detectives. Although she never worked a day in her life and certainly not as an accountant, she retained her well-honed capacity for understanding money and how people with it are able to protect their assets.

Caitlin throws a few more softballs before getting down to the hard stuff.

She pushes Anne off balance by abruptly changing course and asking, "How well do you know Usama ibn al Bakr?"

Anne is stonily quiet for a moment then replies cooly, "Not that well. I am sure we have met. I think he was a client of the bank."

Caitlin ignores the half-true response, "How much do you have to do with the Universal Islamic Assistance Foundation, Mrs. Marcus?"

Anne is aware that both the tone and the formality of the interview have changed. She struggles to remain calm and civil.

"I think I may have attended a fund-raiser or two—rubber chicken affairs. I don't recall having donated much of anything. Howard always took care of that sort of thing."

That is partially a half-truth and partly a full-out lie. Caitlin and Rosalie know for certain that Anne's signature is on almost a dozen large checks made out to the foundation.

"Umm hmmh," Caitlin muses. "Tell us, please, about your San Francisco account. How large is it? Where does the money come from? And where does it go?"

Anne stands up and announces, "That's it for today. I am very tired and cannot tolerate any more stress. Being in this witness protection situation has taken a severe toll on me. I'm sure you understand. The security officer will see you out."

She sees that her two guests are not getting up; so, she abandons the façade of courtesy and walks out of the room.

"That's revealing, no?" Caitlin says.

Chapter Thirteen

The first pair of guards turn the north corner of the rear of the Draguz apartment building and pick their way through the rubble and trash in the rear lot like blind men following a pathway made familiar by repetition. Sybil takes advantage of that aspect of brain function—the mind fills in blanks for vision when vision is limited, but the mind is familiar. The guards move quickly, completely confident in their minds' eye views. Sybil has the team put a large dead branch of a tree directly across the path. The two men walk rapidly into the impediment and crash to the ground cursing from the cuts and scrapes they get from the tangled branches. In two seconds, Ed and two other agents swarm them and render them unconscious with cloths soaked in chloroform. The three agents bind them hand and foot, gag their mouths, and cover their eyes with the all-purpose spy tool—duct tape—and drag them to the back of the lot. They will not awaken before Sybil and her team are long gone, and they will be disoriented and amnesiac when they are finally found.

McGee has been monitoring the front of the building. He clicks his walkie-talkie on and sends the three-click message that the other two guards are standing in their place in front waiting to make their pass around the back.

Ed, Sybil, and one of the female agents remove one of the glass panes of the rear entry door, reach in, unlock it, and in a couple of seconds they are inside. Their night-vision goggles afford them sufficient visibility to be able to make their way to the fifth floor without making a sound. There, they encounter the first of two surprises—the inevitable intervention of Murphy's Law that occurs in every covert operation mission.

Despite their prolonged surveillance of the building and multiple, multiple passes by Mazurkiewicz's apartment room door—which led them to the lulling idea that the hit man had no inside security personnel—there is, in fact, a large, well-armed, and fully alert Bulgarian secret service guard standing there front and center. A frontal attack by the team is untenable. They have to go to plan B.

There is no plan B, and they all slip back into the stairwell to concoct one. Lydia Proxmire, the female CIA covert-ops agent, proposes the only solution that seems at all plausible.

"I can get off the elevator and stagger my drunken way down the hall toward my room, and when I pass by him, I take him out."

"Great plan," Sybil says, "except for a couple of flaws. First of all, that behemoth is twice your size; second of all, you will have lost the element of surprise; and third, you are going to walk down the hall in a ninja-SWAT outfit that will put even the dumbest clod on high alert."

"Thought of all of that. Firstly, I can play the part of a pretty good drunk. Second, I can get out of my ops outfit and carry only my black-blade ceramic knife. Third, I am the match of any man in the martial arts department. Our unit practices four hours every day—hard hit practices. And finally, there will be the element of surprise and diversion. I'll wiggle my butt and shake my upper accruements enticingly—that is an extra-curricular skill I have kept a secret. He will be blinded by my dazzle; and, slam, bam, thank you, Ma'am, I'll put him down."

They all have a quiet laugh at her chutzpah and decide that they cannot come up with anything better. She pulls off her clothing, revealing a set of form-fitting pink long johns. She has a nice form under that fitting outfit, and it could pass as pajamas. She is barefoot.

"Don't peek," she says with a wicked twinkle in her eyes.

Ed places his hands over his eyes with large gaps between the fingers, provoking a second small laugh from the women.

"*Vaya con Dios*," Sybil says.

Lydia gives her teammates a double thumbs-up and tip-toes away down the stairs to the fourth floor. She gets on the elevator and pushes the "five" button. Her nerves and senses are on high alert. Her well-compartmentalized mind brings up the self-defense compartment, and her brain switches to killer Krav Maga combat mode. She will pass the guard on her left; so, she clutches the black knife in her right hand out of sight. The door opens, and she staggers out—a drunken celebrator from some distant party. She looks fetching and available in her cute pink jammies.

The guard turns to look at her with intense hypervigilance and eyes her with high suspicion at first. Then his internal computer sees the slight, voluptuous, ingénue tottering down the hallway toward him. His manness takes over, and he becomes helpless as all men do with the approach of a tantalizing moving visual image—all curves and swaying "accruements." His fight and flight adrenaline rush damps down.

He even makes the first move, "Hi, cutie, what's a nice girl like you doing up at a time like this?"

Of course, he is speaking Bulgarian, of which American Lydia Proxmire does not understand a word.

She gives him a silly but enticing drunken smile and stops directly in front of him and wiggles her "accruements," enough to keep his eyes centered below her clavicles. He looks and reaches to determine for himself if this is a dream or an incredible and unexpected opportunity. From out of the darkness to her right, Lydia arcs her surgically sharp combat knife across the throat of the totally unsuspecting giant. Acting by reflex with his life's blood gushing out in front of him, he lunges at Lydia. His three hundred pound bulk, now dead, collapses on the 135 pound American agent, and they crash to the floor with a good deal more noise that Lydia had hoped. She is pinned underneath the man's inert body and is soaked with four liters of sticky slick blood.

The rest of the team rushes down the hall and is within two feet of Lydia when the second stage of Murphy's Law occurs. In a second surprise of the evening, the apartment door is pulled open and another—very alert, very formidable—guard rushes out. Ed flies across the two bodies on the floor and rams his head into the man's gut, propelling him back into the apartment. For a moment, Ed has the upper hand as the guard struggles to get his breath. The commotion awakens Mazurkiewicz who—by dint of his long training and his basic instincts to survive—is fully ready to enter the fight or to escape, whichever becomes the best option for him.

Sybil has no choice. It is her turn to dredge up her martial arts training. She hurtles past Ed and the guard fighting on the floor and tackles the unarmed, but now fully awake, Mazurkiewicz. He is no novice in the martial arts department, and goes down still completely full of fight. He gets Sybil in the guard position with his strong wiry legs wrapped around her slender waist. She makes a mistake—to underestimate her opponent's skill—and attempts to choke him from her kneeling position—a mistake only a gross novice would make.

Mazurkiewicz throws his right leg up and over her left shoulder and pulls at her right arm to pin it. She realizes her mistake and that she has a couple of nanoseconds to avoid being placed in a triangle hold that will completely incapacitate her, and she will die in ignominy in a dingy apartment in a nothing city in a backwater country. She becomes a wildcat. She leans fully forward and bends her arm at the elbow, preventing him from getting it fully extended and breaking her arm at the joint as he finishes his cruel choking move. He strains to get his leg all the way around behind her neck. Strains too hard.

Sybil summons up all her energy, strength, mobility, and skill and jams her partially entrapped right elbow into his exposed groin. He flinches. She takes advantage and keeps him off balance until she is able to turn him over prone. He makes a mistake then. Instead of maintaining his grip on her wrist, he lets go and struggles up to his knees and elbows. That is the perfect opportunity for Sybil. He has made the novice mistake that violates one of the premier rules of jujitsu— never turn your back on your opponent. His accompanying mistake is to have underestimated Sybil because she is a mere woman, and not a very big one at that.

She does what any Brazilian jujitsu black belt would do: she clamps his exposed neck in the *mata leão* [kill the lion] choke hold. He struggles in vain, knowing that she can kill him with this choke. He manages to turn her over on her back with him supine on top of her. That is a mistake for two reasons. First, it allows a little blood to flow back into his oxygen-starved brain and to cause brain swelling. Second, that position is a better one to increase the purchase of the *mata leão*. Those two mistakes hasten the cessation of blood flow to his swollen brain. Now unconsciousness is inevitable; death can easily follow, and he is powerless to stop it.

Sybil whispers soothingly, "Resistance is futile. It is better to give up all hope."

That is the last thing Byelorussian international killer Viachaslau Mazurkiewicz hears before he slips away into the soft darkness.

Sybil checks. He is not dead, just unconscious, and will remain that way for hours. She quickly directs her attention to the noisy struggle going on between the giant and Ed there on the apartment floor. Ed is losing; and the giant has his beef roast-sized fist ready to smash the smaller man's face, end the fight, kill Ed, and then turn on Sybil. Ed is thrashing about spoiling the guard's aim, but he cannot hold out much longer.

The generous coating of blood has created a slick enough lining between Lydia and the huge corpse smashing her into the floor that she is able to squirm out of her fix. She rolls out and takes a few life returning gulps of air. Her brain clears rapidly, and she can now see Ed's life-threatening predicament. She scrambles to her feet and races into the room and throws her body against the much larger guard, knocking him off balance. He has not nearly lost his advantage and bats Lydia away as if she were a bothersome fly.

Sybil joins Lydia; and, between the two of them, they are able to topple him off Ed. Now it is three little people against one giant. Like the Lilliputians, they are able to turn him onto his back. He is still very nearly a match for the three of them for all of their skills.

Outside, McGee, Mac, and the rest of the team have completed their ambush of the other two outside sentries. Mac takes care of the disposition of their inert, but still living, bodies and sends McGee into the apartment building to see what is keeping Sybil, Ed, and Lydia. He arrives at the door to Mazurkiewicz's apartment just in time to see the giant guard beginning to tip the scales in his favor in his fight with the three CIA agents. His incredible strength is enough to get all three of his opponents turning over, with him about to reassume the superior position. Unfortunately for him, his back his turned to McGee. Fortunately for McGee and the agents, McGee has a sap, and he knows how to use it from his long street experience in New York. He delivers one well-placed blow with the sap to the giant's occiput, and the fight is over.

There is only time for a few heaving breaths before a division of labor sets in. Sybil calls the local CIA "cleaners" who arrive from their van hidden up the street in a matter of minutes. They set about to clean the blood, package the dead man's corpse in a large plastic ground sheet, and to bind and gag the remaining, now unconscious guard. Lydia runs into the apartment's shower and sheds the coating of clotted blood and her once pink, now red, long johns. One of the cleaners hands Lydia a new ninja-SWAT uniform to cover her nakedness. McGee runs back down the four flights of stairs to let Mac and the others know what has transpired.

Sybil, McGee, Ed, and Mac bundle up Mazurkiewicz in a carpet and lug him out of a side door of the building. A second van has been alerted, and they dump the killer's limp body into the back and speed away back to the airport and off on their three-stop odyssey back to the United States.

The "cleaners" are remarkably skilled and efficient at what they do. In fifteen minutes—the time it takes for the local gendarmerie to mobilize—they remove all traces of blood, tidy the room, and load one dead and five living, but unconscious, security guards into their van. Police sirens and lights round the corner of Sveti Kliment Street as the CIA "cleaner" van turns innocuously away onto Han Asparuh Street. It is as close as it is possible to be, but the "cleaners" are used to that. It is part of the pride they take in their work.

Chapter Fourteen
Epilogue

Before McGee, Sybil, and her team can get back to the US with their human trophy, several things fall in place in the Decklin Marcus case; several things go remarkably well; and all-in-all McGee & Associates Investigations is able to consider the case quite successful overall.

On the debit side, Anne Marcus—the murderess who killed her own son to hide her secret collusion with al-Qaeda—is able to convince her minders at Fort Meade to let her go out for an evening of entertainment with two of the other people for whom they have responsibility—a mob accountant and an NSA whistle-blower, who are both slated to testify—one in court and the other before Congress. In the confusion of the carefree dinner and shopping trip, Anne slips away into a shopping mall ladies room and out the window of the restroom. The next—and only time—she is ever seen again is in a security photo on the Island of Nevis—an island which is part of the inner arc of the Leeward Islands chain of the West Indies and has one of the most privacy protective set of banking laws in the world. She is seen smiling in front of one of its myriad banks. By the time international diplomatic negotiations between the island and the United States are complete, Anne's bank balance has been transferred to Vanuatu and on into the mists of obscurity.

On the credit side, Howard Everhart Marcus has a conscience and is utterly devastated by his own and his wife's actions. When he learns that Anne is the contractor for the murder of their only son, he assumes full responsibility for both hers and his part in the terrible and destructive plot. He agrees to divulge the location of all of the money his bank unit illegally transferred and all of his own assets in return—strangely—for the government allowing McGee to be paid in full. He considers McGee to be the only man of his word in the whole affair and wants him to receive his due.

When Sybil gets back with Mazurkiewicz, she takes him to a secure and secret location in the relatively unpopulated portion of Loudoun County, Virginia, where the CIA maintains an ultra-secret, off-the-books interrogation center which Sybil had built during the case of the naval intelligence agency mole. Mazurkiewicz—once he was persuaded of the futility of resisting and of the meager benefits to himself—became an encyclopedia of information about the Russian mafia and its connections with al-Qaeda. As a result, several hundred mobsters and jihadists land in prison and in the embrace of Gitmo. Mazurkiewicz now languishes for the rest of his life known as prisoner #17227-039 in Federal Bureau of Prisons facility, ADX Florence, a federal supermax prison in Florence, Colorado—the meanest prison in America. His life—if one can call it a life—is going to be spent in a windowless, cheerless cell in the solitary confinement.

Caitlin gets a scolding for having prematurely informed Anne that the private investigation firm, the FBI, and the NYPD have the goods on her. The last part of the scolding is the admonition by the boss to "live and learn."

No one is the wiser about Sybil and her covert-ops team's most recent adventure. She finds her inbox to be less full than usual, and arranges to take a short car trip with her husband Charles Daniels and her college-student daughter, Cerisse. The Daniels family has adopted a firm policy of "ask me no questions, and I'll tell you no lies," which seems to work.

McGee's reputation is at its zenith, and the firm attracts a fascinating and potentially very lucrative new client—a whistle-blower from a dictatorial religious cult—which may turn out to be a major tort case with McGee, Ivory, and Caitlin as the principal investigators.

-The End-